F IS FOR FAKE MARRIAGE

ANNIE J. ROSE

CHAPTER 1

TOBY

Paris had had more of an effect on me than I thought it would. Back home in New York, I got accustomed to the way Maddie made me feel. Telling myself a relationship in the office was a terrible idea, I got used to the tug in my stomach when I saw her leaned over a table and the shiver of desire when she smiled at me. It was a constant state of attraction that simmered just beneath the surface, and I never once acted on it. I doubted she even knew what I was feeling. At least, she hadn't known for long.

But then the marketing team decided to do the photo-shoots for our most recent campaign in Paris. The City of Lights was widely considered the most romantic place in the world. It was perfect for the fresh, modern, and edgy marketing campaign we wanted for the app I'd developed. It was a suggestion of Jane, the newest member of the marketing department, that we all started envisioning the pictures being taken on the streets of Paris. The sketches she drew for the campaign were impressive enough to catch the attention of Nik Nygard, the wealthy businessman who recently merged my company into his. She had a vision for the campaign, and it was nothing short of extraordinary. Compelling and instantly influential, it combined the dynamic, contemporary edge with the history and fantasy dreamscape of Paris. It was exactly what we needed to create a launch for my app that would take the world by storm.

When we first started talking about taking the trip, my mind was completely on the photographs and how they would work with the rest of the campaign we planned. It wasn't long before I started thinking about spending the time there with Maddie. I knew it wouldn't be easy being surrounded by the romantic aura of the city. I knew it would be even more difficult when I heard we wouldn't be staying in several hotel rooms, but all sharing one large apartment so we would be close together. Sharing the space with her and knowing she was so close was going to make my attraction to her even more difficult to resist, but I thought I could do it. I thought I'd be strong enough to push those feelings down and focus completely on work.

Obviously, I was wrong. As my fingers combed back through her glossy hair and my mouth eagerly sucked her plush bottom lip in between my own, I knew my expecta- tions of myself were far off. There was no way I was going to be able to get through this trip without getting my hands on her. I needed to taste her, feel her body, and hold her in my arms. My control held out almost the entire week. Being on a breakneck schedule that kept us running essentially from the moment we got up until we fell on our faces asleep at night helped, but that didn't stop the dirty thoughts and longing looks. I lusted after Maddie from the day I hired her and being in such close quarters with her condensed all those thoughts and feelings down into an intense need I couldn't resist.

The connection between us grew throughout the week. Stolen glances and shared smiles turned to small touches when no one was looking, brushing up against each other accidentally on purpose, and me finding as many ways as possible to work even more closely with her. Every day I found new ways to be near her and all those tiny moments finally erupted. The night before we stayed up late after the others went to bed, but instead of working, we ended up making out furiously on the couch.

It wasn't enough because it only made us hungrier for each other, and it was all I could do to get to the end of the day. We stayed as close as possible to each other through the photoshoot, touched at every chance we got, and even made it through lunch pressed close together at a tiny table. Nik's invitation for us all to go to a celebratory dinner together was the last straw. Slipping into the back of a cab, we were barely out of sight of the cafe where we left Jane and Nik before we were tangled together. The excuses we gave them were weak, but neither of us could stand the thought of wasting our last night in Paris. If there was ever going to be a moment when we would give in to the boiling heat between us, this was it.

And we weren't letting a second slip through our fingers. The night before, Maddie broke us apart and told me we had to stop. She reminded me that a relationship between us was against company policy. It was enough to stop us then, but as soon as we saw each other that morning, we couldn't keep our hands off each other. Sneaking in the touches on each other throughout the day when no one was watching only made me hotter and needier, and I knew I couldn't hold out much longer. Now we'd finally made an excuse to get away from Nik and Jane and were alone together. I was finally going to have her. Maddie and I were going to make passionate love, and I couldn't be more excited.

I wasn't going to let myself think about anything but this moment. I pushed aside what she'd said to me the night before and any concerns that lingered in my mind. We weren't in New York. We weren't in the office, and nobody else was around. This was the romance and fantasy of Paris, and we were letting it take over. I wanted her more than I had ever wanted anything or anyone, and I was willing to ignore reality to enjoy her for as long as I had the chance.

In the seconds between me getting into the cab and kissing Maddie, I gave the driver an address. When we pulled up in front of the hotel, it was just as beautiful and elegant as I hoped. And that's what Maddie deserved. Even if I could only be with her for one night, I wanted to give her everything I could.

I got out of the cab and reached in to help her out. After paying the driver, I wrapped my arm around Maddie's waist and hurried her inside. She leaned against me at the counter as I checked in, asking for their best suite. The clerk eyed us, then glanced down at our hands as if looking for luggage. We didn't have any, and she gave a knowing smile before handing over the key. I took it gratefully, and Maddie and I rushed across the lobby to the elevator. The ride seemed to take forever. I forced myself not to push her up against the wall and start undressing her right there.

When the doors finally opened, I took Maddie's hand and we headed down the hallway together. She stopped me after a few feet and pulled me to her for another deep kiss before scurrying away. I chased after her, grabbing her from behind and spinning her around in my arms to kiss her again. She laughed as we continued toward our room. Finally, we made it to the door, and I swiped the key card. It opened and we tumbled through together.

At last, we were alone together behind a closed and locked door. The silence was thrilling. Finally, blessed privacy.

I put my hands on Maddie's waist and leaned in for another kiss, but she pulled back. Her deep blue eyes locked on mine, and she stared at me intently, as if making sure I was paying careful attention to what she was going to say.

"Remember, this is just tonight. A one-time fling," she said.

"I know," I told her, nodding as I leaned toward her again.

Maddie flattened her hand in the middle of my chest and pushed me back again.

"And when we get back to New York, it's like it never happened. We go right back to the way we were before we came here. Working alongside each other and nothing else," she reiterated.

"Yes," I told her, nodding again as I swallowed down the doubts of my ability to actually stop desiring her whether we were in New York or not.

My confirmation was enough for Maddie. She threw her arms around my neck and kissed me passionately. I wrapped my arms around her and pulled her up hard against me. Lifting her off her feet, I carried her over to the bed and set her down on the end of the mattress. Getting down on my knees in front of her, I lifted one foot and took off her shoe, and then took off the other. I moved forward, pushing her thighs apart so I could gather her against me again. Our mouths met and we kissed for another few seconds before I pulled back to continue undressing her.

Using my fingers to gather her shirt, I pulled the hem from the waistband of her pants and slid my hands up her to feel the ripple of her rib cage beneath her skin. Maddie lifted her arms, and I pushed the shirt up and off. Her pale pink bra perfectly cupped her full breasts, and I leaned down to nuzzle my face between them. Her soft skin was flushed and felt warm against my lips. I swept my tongue across one slope and then the other as Maddie's fingers dug into my hair. She pressed her hips forward to grind harder against my chest.

Bringing my mouth back to hers, I kissed her deeply and released the button of her pants. The zipper went down, and she lifted her hips so I could pull the tight jeans from her hips and down her legs. Backing up as I went, I tugged them the rest of the way off and tossed them aside. Maddie grabbed the front of my shirt and pulled me up to my feet in front of her. Sliding to the very edge of the bed, she went to work on my belt, then the button and zipper of my pants. As she took them down, I stepped out of my shoes and threw my shirt over to join her clothes.

I wrapped one arm around her waist and scooped her up so I could move us both higher on the bed. My body stretched out over hers, and our mouths crushed against each other. Maddie moaned into my mouth, and her hips rocked beneath me. In one movement, I rolled over onto my back and positioned her to straddle me. She reached behind and unhooked her bra. The lacy fabric popped away from her body, and I groaned as I lifted my hands to massage into her soft, bare breasts.

Her nipples tightened beneath my touch, pressing into my palms. Maddie arched into my hands and moved her hand behind her to run her hand over the bulge of my hardening erection. I looped my thumbs in the waistband of my boxers to shuck them, and she raised her hips to let me move her panties out of the way. She sat back and stretched her legs out, letting me lead the damp scrap of fabric off her feet. She started to tuck her legs back under her, but I stopped her, holding them in place, then pressing her thighs apart. I bent my knees so she could lean back on them and paused to let my eyes rove over her, taking in every gorgeous inch of her body.

I touched my hand to the middle of her chest and drew it down her belly to her navel. My fingertip dipped down into it before continuing down to her hip bones. Her head fell back, and her muscles trembled as I traced my fingers from one hip over to the other. My touch moved back and forth, sweeping lower with each pass. She gasped and her thighs opened a little farther, inviting me to touch her. It didn't take much coaxing. I let my hand trail down the rest of her stomach and finally found her slick, wet heat.

CHAPTER 2

MADDIE

My mouth opened and I drew in a sharp breath at the feeling of Toby's fingers slipping across my already taut, sensitive peak. The chemistry between us and the slow burn of the week together kept my body in a perpetual state of arousal, and now the need was paying off. It was obvious Toby could feel how ready I was for his touch. He groaned when he felt the slickness of my body across his fingers, and the sound only increased the rush. Toby swirled his fingertips around my clit, using pressure so perfect it was like he already knew every detail of my body. The wave of intense pleasure sent a thrill through my body that settled right between my thighs.

The position he put me in was completely new, and the experience of it almost overwhelmed me. I'd never been that free and open with a man. Facing him with my thighs open and my legs on either side of him, I should have felt vulnerable and exposed, but I didn't. There was no hesitation or embarrassment. I didn't want to cover up or reposition myself so he couldn't see me. I relished the feeling of his eyes drinking me in. I wanted him to memorize every inch of me and build the intensity I felt low in my belly. I wanted Toby to feel the same powerful draw I was experiencing and crave a connection so explosive it would leave both of us unable to forget it, even as we put it behind us.

He explored me further, tracing every curve and dip until I was shaking with anticipation. When his fingers sank into me, my body lit up and I cried out. My hips pushed down against his hand, wanting more of him. It wasn't enough just to have that feeling. I needed more.

Toby turned his hand and settled the pad of his thumb onto my clit again. The combination of his fingers sliding slowly against my inner walls and his thumb applying just the perfect pressure to my intensely sensitive pearl sent me instantly spiraling. There was no way I was going to be able to maintain my control for long. He was pushing me to levels of pleasure I'd never experienced, and I didn't want to miss any of it. Closing my eyes, I let my head fall back and my thighs completely open. My hips rocked against his hand almost involuntarily, my body completely taking over. Tension starting building in the tips of my fingers and the bottoms of my feet. Heat burned across my face, and my muscles shook and trembled.

I didn't try to hold back. I let the power of the feelings rush through me, and my orgasm set my body aflame. Toby held his fingers deep inside me and pressed the other hand to the frantic beating of my heart as I rode the waves of climax. I could feel his thick, hard cock pressing against my back, and even as I came down from the intense peak, I knew I wasn't done. I wanted so much more.

Reading my mind, he lowered his legs, scooped me up against him, and rolled me onto my back. We landed with his hips nestled between my thighs and the tip of his hard cock nudging my still-tingling opening. I wrapped my arms around his neck and pulled him down for a kiss. As our mouths played across each other, Toby positioned his hips and eased forward. The sensation of him filling me fully and completely was even better than I could have imagined. I clung to him, wanting every bit of my body to touch his. There was a dizzying, almost indescribable feeling of desperation mixed with the fulfillment. Like he was everything and yet I couldn't get enough.

Toby held himself in place for only a few seconds before his hips started to move. His thrusts were strong and insistent, but not demanding or forceful. They let me concentrate on the delicious glide of him across every intimate bit, discovering places no one had ever touched. The first climax softened and heated my body, so I was ready to accept all of him, and Toby didn't relent.

Just when I thought I couldn't get any more pleasure, he lifted one of my legs and propped it on his shoulder. Holding himself up on his hands on either side of me for leverage, he created a new angle that delivered a wave of deeper, more explosive sensations. I held on to his shoulders and kissed him eagerly. Our bodies found a rhythm, and everything else in the world disappeared around us. Even as Toby ran a trail of kisses down the side of my neck and brushed the tip of his tongue across my skin, I could hardly wrap my head around what was happening. I couldn't believe I was having sex with my boss, but at the same time, I couldn't help myself. This was too incredible. There was no way I was letting my logic get in the way and stop me from tumbling down this delirious whirlpool.

Toby's grunts and groans got louder and more intense as he picked up speed. Our bodies climbed together, and I could feel the rush of another climax coming through my body. We held on tight to each other, and at the same moment my body crashed, and his cock pulsed and throbbed inside me. Each tight clench of my walls drew him deeper, milking him and connecting us more. I clawed at his back, and he bit down on my bottom lip until we both finally collapsed, gasping for breath. His skin was slick with sweat, and I tasted some of it, enjoying the saltiness on my tongue. Toby nuzzled his head into the curve of my neck and shoulder and kissed the tender spot there. One hand trailed along my side, then slipped beneath me to gather me close so he could fall to the side and curl around me.

We lay there silently for several long minutes, our hands lazily tracing across slick skin and our mouths occasionally finding each other for languid kisses. Our breaths slowed and calmed as our bodies drifted down from the peak and settled back to normal. There was no need to say anything. Not at that moment. It was enough to just be in the bubble with him. I was surprised by how good it felt to just lie there in his arms. I didn't want to move, didn't want anything else but to feel the warmth of his skin and listen to his breath and heartbeat.

He was truly a remarkable man. I wouldn't admit it to him, but that was a fairly new revelation for me. I wasn't immediately enraptured by him or as impressed as other people seemed to be. When I first went to him to interview for the job in the marketing department of his company, he didn't seem all that special. If anything, it was frustrating to see his success. I thought he was nothing more than a computer nerd who'd stumbled into a business and was now had everything he could have ever dreamed of dropped right in his lap. Then he'd hired me, and the more we worked together, the more I learned about him.

I realized my initial impression of him wasn't at all the

truth. Toby worked hard for everything he had. He was very smart and extremely good at what he did, but he was also compassionate and funny. He really cared about the people around him and wanted to make sure he was creating a company that benefitted more than just him. He was really a great catch. Too bad he was my boss and I'd have to let him go.

That thought coming into my mind and swelling until it took up every corner and recess was enough to sour the afterglow. The bubble around us burst, and I had to face reality again. Letting out a sigh, I peeled myself away from Toby and climbed out of the bed. If I let myself lie there for another few seconds, I would want to be there for the rest of the night, and that just wasn't something we could do. It was better to end it now so we didn't get any deeper.

Toby's fingertips brushed along my lower back as he reached for me, but I forced myself to ignore the touch and get up. My clothes were scattered around the room, and I walked around, gathering them up. I could feel his eyes on me. It seemed strange, but the feeling of that look was different now. There was a distinct separation between the way it felt when he looked at me for the first time, seeing my body presented to him, and now that we'd fully experienced each other. It was deeper and more intense, and I could feel it on me even as I walked into the bathroom to put myself back together.

Several minutes later, I came back out. He was still lying in bed, covered to his hips with a sheet as he reclined on the pillows. It was an enticing scene, and I was almost tempted enough to peel off my clothes again and crawl back in with him. Instead, I concentrated on putting on my shoes.

"You don't have to rush off," Toby said from the bed.

I put on my second shoe and straightened, trying to fluff my hair back up.

"Nik and Jane will be waiting for us," I reminded him. "They went to dinner, and they think each of us were off doing different things, but they aren't going to think they'll take all night."

Some of the sleepy contentment disappeared from his face as that sank in. Toby started to flip the sheet back so he could stand up, but I waved him away.

"You don't need to get up, yet. Just relax for a while. Order some room service or something," I told him.

Toby looked at me strangely. "What?"

"We're supposed to be in two different places, remember? It wouldn't look good for the two of us to show back up at the apartment together. We should leave separately and arrive at different times," I said.

He nodded. "Oh. Yeah, that makes sense."

"Great. I'll go first." Suddenly, things got awkward. This wasn't exactly a moment I'd thought all the way through when tangled up in the back of the cab with Toby. "Um. Thanks for the great time tonight."

I cringed and turned away, heading for the door as fast as I could without breaking out into a full run. I didn't need to hear whatever he was going to come up with to answer the absurd stream of words that just tumbled out of my mouth. Hurrying through the lobby, I didn't make eye contact with anyone, especially not the clerk at the desk who had known exactly why we were checking in. There was mercifully a cab already waiting at the front of the hotel, and I dove inside it.

The driver looked at me in the rearview mirror, and I gave him the address of the apartment. Dropping my head back against the headrest, I stared at the ceiling of the cab and silently chastised myself. Embarrassment burned on my face and chest the entire drive through the city. Like I expected, the cab stopped on a side road rather than actually going to the front of the apartment. The entrance was down a narrow cobblestone road off an alley too tight for cars to go down comfortably. Somehow, climbing out of the cab and taking the walk to the apartment just made my embarrassment worse.

As soon as I got inside the apartment, I hurried to the bathroom. I took a long, hot shower and got into my favorite baggy pajamas before stuffing myself under my covers and pulling them up to my chin. I squeezed my eyes closed, but it wasn't any use. An hour later I still couldn't sleep as the memories of what happened with Toby replayed through my head over and over again.

CHAPTER 3

TOBY

It was amazing how much could change in less than a year. I was a theme that had repeated itself several times recently in my life, but seven months after coming back from the business trip in Paris, the differences were more pronounced. Not all of them were bad. Being back in New York was comfortable. It was home and familiar, unlike the streets of Paris which didn't seemed completely real despite how long we spent there. The highlight of those seven months was definitely the launch of the new ad campaign. We worked ourselves into the ground in the days and weeks after getting back to make sure every detail was put in place. The final result of the photoshoot and Jane's artwork was nothing short of spectacular. It was far more than I ever could have imagined, and even Nik was impressed. That was no minor feat. When it came to marketing and creating a company image, Nik Nygard had seen it all, done it all, and probably pioneered the vast majority of it.

But Jane took him by surprise, creating a layered marketing approach that appealed to a massive range of consumers across various mediums. It was a tremendous amount of work, and the anxiety leading up to the launch was real. Everything balanced on that campaign. My company had already been around for several years, but I hadn't been able to make much of it. Catching Nik's attention and having him agree to merge with me and boost my app was a once-in-a-lifetime dream, but just having his name behind my software wasn't enough to really make it a success. It was all centered on how well we could reach out to the target demographic and convince them to accept my company. This ad campaign was my one shot. If it was successful, it could launch my company into massive success and get the momentum rolling so I could keep growing. If it failed, everything I'd worked so hard for would crumble around me.

Fortunately, it was an instant and astonishing hit. What wasn't so fortunate was Jane not being around to enjoy it with us. She resigned a few weeks after we all got back to New York, and the office was definitely feeling the loss of the marketing department's star employee. It was affecting Maddie particularly hard. The two of them had grown close working together, and Maddie seemed sad not having her friend around every day. Some of the spark was sucked out of her, and she didn't seem as motivated without Jane to bounce ideas off. It was hard to see her that way, especially because I couldn't say anything to her. She did her best to cover it up and never said anything outright.

I only noticed because I wasn't even close to being over her. We agreed in Paris we weren't going to acknowledge anything between us when we got home. We were taking a Vegas approach to the whole situation. What happened there, stayed there, and that's just the way it was. This was far easier said than done. We hadn't said a word to each other about our night together since the plane touched down, but that didn't mean I wasn't thinking about it. Maddie wasn't so easy to compartmentalize. I held my thoughts and feelings to myself, but I still lusted after her obsessively. She filled my mind, dominated my thoughts. I watched her from a distance, keeping an eye on her, but maintaining our professional relationship just as we agreed.

Her sadness after Jane left was difficult to deal with. The entire marketing department shifted when she left, and much of the enthusiasm was gone from the meetings and the work we were doing. There were a few times when Ethan, the director of the department, tried to find someone to replace her, but was quickly proven futile. No one had the vision and talent Jane did, and even those who came close didn't fit in the way she had. We just had to carry on without her.

It wasn't just Jane's departure and the slowdown in the marketing department that was different than before we left for Paris. Nik had been an absolute bear lately. Not that he was exactly known for being soft and cuddly, but he was harsher and more temperamental than usual. It seemed things weren't going well with his ex-wife. I personally didn't see many circumstances when things could go well with an ex suddenly showing up and moving into your house, but his attitude had gotten progressively worse.

I couldn't help but wonder if maybe Nik had a thing for Jane as well. He never said anything, and his response to her leaving had been more diplomatic. But the man did quietly have several of the ad campaign sketches Jane drew framed and hung up in his office. He said it was just because they were beautiful, and they represented the first successful campaign the merged companies did together. I didn't know if I fully bought that. It was such a personal thing. He didn't hang the pictures in the conference room or down the hallway. They were right there in his office, close by him all day.

Shoving the conspiracy theory out of my mind, I told myself I was being silly. My mentor was far too straitlaced of a businessman to fool around with an employee. Unlike me.

I was definitely not immune to my employees. And it was proving more than obvious that afternoon as I tried to get through a meeting reviewing quarterly figures on the success of the marketing campaign. I struggled to concentrate on the dry rambling of facts and figures. I had the basic idea of it down. The share price was way up, and at last time I checked, I saw the app was getting a ton of downloads. I assumed everything was going well. There wasn't much other involvement necessary from me. I was there essentially as a figurehead. It gave me an excuse to let my mind wander, but I had to be careful. I didn't want to get caught staring at Maddie. That was a considerable challenge when she was just a conference table away from me.

She was so beautiful. I never got tired of looking at her. It would seem like I'd be used to her by now. More than a year of watching her, staring at her, memorizing her every feature. I should have been used to looking at her, but I wasn't. It was like every time I saw her, she was more compelling. Looking at her brought to mind the memories of us in Paris, her body naked and sweating beneath mine. Just a glance her way made me hard. The thoughts of my hands running over her curves, my lips gathering her taste, and my cock sinking deep into her tormented me. Memories of the sounds that tumbled out of her and surrounded me in that luxurious hotel room were sweet torture, and I would have given anything to be able to repeat it. I told myself, and Maddie, it was just a one-time thing. But that night in Paris, I actually believed it. I thought I would be able to indulge myself and my powerful cravings for her, and then the urges would go away. This night was supposed to carry me through and let me put it all behind us when we got home.

But that was far from how it actually worked out. Now that I'd had a real taste of her, I was desperate for more. It was the difference between looking through a bakery window at something that looked delicious and actually sampling the decadent pastry. One was a want, a fantasy that came from just thinking about how good it could be. The other became a gnawing craving that came from knowing just how incredible it was and needing more. Maddie was that need. I couldn't look at her without thinking about what her body felt like beneath her clothes. I couldn't listen to her talk without thinking about her mouth against my lips and her tongue tangled with mine.

I didn't know what she was thinking or how she was feeling. But that day, I noticed a strain in her eyes that wasn't there before. It wasn't just the sadness that had been there since Jane left. It was something more, and I couldn't just let it slide. No matter what was going on between us, I was worried about her and wanted to make sure she was all right. As the meeting ended, I lingered back and waited for the others to leave. Maddie gave me a tight smile and was staring out of the room when I took hold of her arm and pulled her to the side.

"Hi," I said, not sure really where to start.

"Hey, Toby. Did you need something?" she asked.

It was a loaded question, but I forced myself past it.

"I just haven't talked to you in a while. How have you been?" Now that I was closer to her, I examined her face and saw the strain was even more pronounced. "You look tired."

She made a face at my bluntness, then gave a wry smile.

"Maybe I am tired," she answered.

"Is it the campaign? Did it wipe you out? Maybe you should take some time off," I suggested.

I thought I was being considerate and offering her some time to recharge after all the hard work we put into the campaign, but Maddie didn't seem to take it that way. A look of panic flashed through her eyes. An instant later, she disguised it, shaking her head and glancing away as she adjusted the strap of her satchel over her shoulder.

"Taking time off is the last thing I need right now," she told me.

The answer worried me, and I rested a hand on her shoulder.

"I'm always here, you know. If you ever need to talk."

Maddie glanced at the door, then turned a bright smile to me. It was like she was trying to drown out all the tension and negative emotion in the glare of that smile.

"I'm fine," she said. "Don't worry."

I frowned as she walked away, not convinced, and upset she wasn't more willing to open up to me. I resented the wall that formed between us and wished we could go back to the camaraderie we had in Paris. We were a team then, playing off each other, finishing each other's thoughts, building each other up when we thought we were too exhausted to keep pushing through the intense schedule. Now it was like we barely knew each other.

Work dragged late into the evening, but as I was getting ready to leave, I noticed the light glowing in another office. Apparently, I wasn't working as late as Nik. I walked up to his office and knocked on the partially open door. Glancing inside, I was expecting Nik hunched over his desk, buried in work like he usually was. Instead, I was surprised to see him drinking a glass of bourbon as he muttered a string of profanity and stared at what looked like a newspaper clipping.

Not bothering to wait for an invitation, I walked into the office and up to the desk.

"Nik? What are you doing?" I asked.

"You should never wait to go after the thing you want, Toby. Because before you know it, it could be gone," Nik told me.

"Are you talking about Angela?" I asked.

Nik grimaced at the sound of his ex-wife's name and shook his head.

"She is the same mistake she always was," he told me.

Without further elaboration, he stood. Scooping up the newspaper clipping, he knocked back the last of his drink and set the glass down hard on his desk.

"I'm taking some time off," he told me as he headed for his office door.

"Taking time off?" I asked, surprised by the uncharacteristic announcement. "Where are you going?"

"To Paris," he muttered.

I looked down at his hand and caught a glimpse of the newspaper clipping. In it I saw Jane's face smiling back through a picture positioned beside the picture of a man I didn't recognize. It occurred to me I was looking at an engagement announcement, and I put two and two together. The musing I thought was silly was true. Nik and Jane.

I suddenly saw my mentor in a whole new light. Maybe he wasn't as straitlaced as I thought.

CHAPTER 4

Multitasking is exceptionally overrated. People are expected to be able to do thirty things at the same time. Never break a sweat, and look good doing it. At least, that's what magazines and TV commercials would lead you to believe. What they don't show is moments like the one that evening when I juggled four grocery bags, tried not to let the overweight purse that slipped from my shoulder buckle my elbow, struggled to unlock the door to my apartment, and cursed like a sailor when my phone started ringing.

Damn those glossy women who can do it all.

It wasn't lost on me that the cursing thought was fairly ironic considering my job in the marketing department meant I was responsible for a wide variety of similar unrealistic advertising campaigns.

"Hold on," I said to the phone.

Of course, it kept ringing. One of these days, someone was going to invent a phone that could understand when someone yelled that from across the room and transmit it to the caller. Until then, people with full hands all over would continue shouting fruitlessly at their ringing phones.

"Hold on," I said again.

My grocery bags were threatening to fall out of my arms, and my purse was on its way to my wrist, but I managed to shove the key in the lock and get the door open. Finally inside, I hauled my groceries into the kitchen and tossed them onto the counter along with my purse. I fumbled for my phone and answered it without bothering to glance at the screen.

"Hello?"

"Well, don't sound so happy to hear from me."

The giggle told me it was Megan. I frowned. My younger sister had been calling a lot recently. Far more than she ever had before. It both worried and annoyed the hell out of me. Megan was the golden child in the eyes of my parents. Always their favorite, the baby of the family was unabashedly spoiled, got away with everything, and was given far more opportunities in life than I ever was. My parents always said they thought I was going to be an only child, but she was their surprise. A bonus baby. Which meant she got all the indulgence and permissiveness I didn't. But that didn't stop Megan from feeling like she needed me to weigh in on and approve of every aspect of her life.

I loved my sister and we were close, but somehow me moving to New York made Megan even needier. I was used to her asking my opinion about everything and needing me to give her words of encouragement whenever she made a decision. She even chose to go to college at Kansas U, my alma mater, because she said if it was good enough for me, it was good enough for her. But since I left home and moved to the city, her clinginess had reached a whole new level. It was particularly worrisome considering she was right at a major turning point in her life.

In her senior year of college, Megan really should have been concentrating on finding a good internship and getting ready to graduate. She should have been looking ahead to the years after the dorm and class schedules to when she would need a job to support herself and couldn't always rely on our father to send her extra cash when she needed it. Instead, I wasn't even sure my little sister knew how many credits she still needed to earn to graduate, let alone had any leads for an internship. Right at the time when she should be finding as many ways as she could to build and polish her resume to appeal to the competitive workforce, she probably didn't even have one.

"What is it, Megan?" I asked.

I propped the phone between my shoulder and my ear so I could start unpacking my groceries. I highly doubted my sister was in enough of a personal crisis to justify my pint of butter pecan melting all over the counter.

"You would not believe what happened to me last night, Maddie," Megan said.

"I probably would," I started, but it wasn't enough to stop her.

Once Megan was on a roll with one of her stories, little could stop her.

"It was so funny. Oh, my gosh. Okay, listen. Are you listening? You have to listen. So, Ashley, Brandy, Jessica, and Sage were getting so fucking serious about their school-work and studying and shit..."

"Aren't you getting ready for exams?" I asked.

"It was just ridiculous. They didn't want to do anything. They were just holed up in their rooms reading books and writing papers and doing flashcards. Can you even believe that? Seriously, how much reading can you actually do? At some point, your brain just has to fill up too much and start rejecting anything. So, honestly, I was doing them a favor…"

"I'm sure you were." I opened up my ice cream and pulled a spoon out of the drawer. This was going to take more than just listening.

"I totally had enough of just sitting around waiting for anything to happen…"

"You could have been studying."

"So, I decided we were going out for the night. You should have seen my dress. I'm going to have to send you a picture of it. It's silver and glittery and has a slit all the way up to my hip. It's so hot. You would look amazing in it. Oh, my gosh! You should come visit me! You can borrow the dress, and I'll bring you out dancing. You're always working. That's all you ever want to talk about. The office, your projects, going after the promotion. Blah, blah, blah…"

"It's what adults do." Along with leaning against the kitchen counter eating ice cream right out of the container.

"You need to relax. Anyway, I detoured. Back to the story. I went and got them and dragged their asses out of the dorm to this amazing frat party I heard about. Of course, they bitched about it at first, but once they got there, it was on. They finally got their heads out of the damn books and started having fun. We had a couple of drinks and started dancing. Then Sage saw this guy who she's been trying to get with all semester. He's this ridiculously hot football player who's in her Lit class. Or her History class. Something. Doesn't matter. She's been drooling on this man for weeks but hasn't had the guts to try anything on him. She keeps saying she's waiting for him to notice her and make the moves because that's so much more romantic. Such bullshit. And I told her so. I'm tired of listening to her mope around and whine because she's doing her best to put out the fall-in-love-with-me vibes when she should just be putting out the come-fuck-me vibes..."

"Those are two completely different things, Megan." I'd gotten through a good portion of the ice cream and decided I should probably cut myself off. Justifying it as dairy and protein from the nuts could really only take me so far.

"It took three Jell-O shots to get through to her, but she finally decided she was going to go after him. But he was already dancing with some chick with bad hair extensions, who couldn't stand up on her shoes. ..."

"Megan..."

I seriously couldn't take the rambling and irrelevant details anymore.

"Megan, stop."

Her voice petered out. "Huh?"

"I've already heard this story," I told her.

"How is that possible? It just happened last night," she pointed out.

"Yeah, I'm aware. And you drunk-dialed me at two in the morning while everyone was trying to pry Sage out from under the air mattress, beer cans, and half-conscious drunk guy. Remember?"

There was a pause.

"No. I don't remember that at all," my sister finally said.

"It's been happening a couple times a week, Megan. And you never remember doing it. Doesn't that tell you something? You really need to stop partying and focus on passing your classes so you can graduate," I told her.

"Are you seriously climbing on my back right now? All I wanted to do was let loose and have some fun. This whole college thing isn't as easy for me as it was for you, Maddie. You aren't even here to help me, and I was never smart.

You know things don't just come to me the way they do for you. I was always nervous about going to college, and I chose the one you went to because I figured you'd be able to help me. Then you up and left. So now what I am supposed to do?"

It was a hissy fit I'd heard before. Whenever I called her out for her behavior, she resorted to sending me on a guilt trip because I took control of my life and moved to New York rather than staying in place to hold her hand through college.

"I did what adults do. I worked hard throughout school to get where I wanted to go and give me the best prospects. I had to move to pursue the career I always wanted. That's what you should be doing. You should be focusing on your own career prospects," I told her.

She let out a sigh that was just as spoiled and melodramatic as the rest of the story.

"It's too hard. I don't know where I'm supposed to look for an internship. I'm not even sure what being an intern is. Somebody offered me a position and then said they weren't even going to pay me. Can you believe that?" she asked.

"Yes, Megan. That's what internships are." I finished putting away my groceries and folded the bags to tuck away in my pantry.

"See? I don't get any of this. I can't figure out how resumes work. I don't know what I'm supposed to say in an interview. I can't stand the clothes people think are professional."

I'd reached my threshold of tolerance for her whining and cut her off.

"Okay, stop. I have to go make dinner. So, if there's nothing more important for you to talk about…"

Megan let out a huff, and I could almost see her with

her arms crossed over her chest and her bottom lip puffing out.

"For your information, I did call for a reason. Not just to chat. I have a message to pass on."

"What's the message?" I said, sighing.

"Coach Shelton will see you real soon. He's got a big question to ask you," Megan said, rattling it off as if she were reading it off a sheet of paper.

My stomach turned and a sick feeling washed over me at the mention of my ex, Craig.

"Where did you get that message?" I asked. "I told you. You need to stay away from Shelton."

Megan laughed. "And there you go, overreacting as always. All right, I've got to go. There's a party tonight, and I need to get ready."

My little sister hung up even as I protested the party and Shelton, and I let out a frustrated growl, throwing down my phone. My mind was reeling. Craig was coming to New York? Why the hell would he do that? And even more important, what would he have to ask me? The thoughts created a tight ball of fear that formed low in my belly and spiked up until it made my heart pound. I still remembered clearly how badly he reacted to our breakup. I was still terrified of him and his abusive behavior. The awful things he did to me throughout our relationship and in the messy aftermath still haunted me.

CHAPTER 5

TOBY

There are many things I loved about my career. In a lot of ways, I was cut out to be a businessman and run a company on a trajectory toward staggering success. And in other ways, I hated it and still wanted to just be tooling around developing my software and not having to deal with day-to-day shit. Conference calls being the perfect example. There was something about having to sit in my office staring at a phone while various voices came out of it that got under my skin. It was harder to concentrate when the people weren't actually in the room with me, and I found my mind wandering more often. It also always seemed like the calls dragged on much longer than an in-person meeting about the same thing.

That was definitely the case as the call I started that afternoon finally gasped to an end. It ran on much later than I expected it to, and everyone had already left by the time I was able to gather my things and head home. I pulled out my phone and started ordering dinner so I could pick it up on the way. Halfway down the hallway, I heard something that sound like somebody muttering. That's not something I expected to hear in an office I thought was empty. I paused and listened. The sound got louder and more distinct. It was definitely a voice, and it didn't sound happy.

I made my way toward it, and the words rose up into a stream of shouted profanity. I knew the voice before I got to the break room. It was Maddie. The angry, increasingly loud cursing worried me, and I rushed to the room, shoving my phone in my pocket. I burst in and found her standing at the counter, yelling angrily at the coffee machine as it sputtered and bubbled ground-filled coffee down the front of the cabinets. It was briefly funny, but she seemed truly agitated rather than just being upset about the machine. Her face was drawn, her expression exhausted and stressed. My chest constricted as the worry for her returned. I stepped up closer to her.

"Maddie?"

She jumped and whipped around. When she saw me, she pressed her hand to the center of her chest, and she drew in a breath.

"Toby. You scared the hell out of me," she said.

"I'm sorry. Do you need help with the coffee machine? You seem to be holding your own against it, but it might get a second wind anytime now."

She didn't seem amused by my teasing and just shook her head, looking back at the malfunctioning maker.

"I don't know what happened. I make coffee every day. Every day I come in here and make coffee. Then tonight it decided to be a little bitch and spit at me," she told me.

Part of me really wanted to laugh, but I held it in. Instead, I walked up to the counter and turned the coffee machine off.

"Maddie, go on home. You've clearly had a long day, and you look exhausted," I said.

She shook her head. "I really don't feel like going home."

"Why is that?" I asked.

She stared down the coffee machine and the mess it made like she was contemplating cleaning it up. She knew as well as I did the cleaning crew would be at the office at midnight, but usually she was adamant about cleaning up after herself and not making their job any more challenging. Apparently, that night she was using up all the goodwill, throwing away her own trash created and giving up on the sludgy mess. Letting out a sigh, she turned on her heel.

"Good night," she said as she started toward the door.

As she tried to get past me, I reached out and took her by her arm. She paused and I gently guided her back in front of me. She didn't fight with me, but her eyes remained off to the side.

"I've had enough of the mysteriousness," I told her. "I want to know what's going on."

"Nothing is going on," she said.

"Cut the bullshit, Maddie," I said. My harsh tone startled her, and her eyes snapped to me. "I want to know what's going on. Clearly you're having a rough time."

"It's nothing for you to worry about," she told me.

"Actually, it is," I said. "As the head of this company, it's my responsibility to look after my team. I need to be sure my employee isn't experiencing a hardship."

It wasn't entirely true but putting my concern behind the veil of my position at least kept our relationship in the professional realm she wanted, but it didn't convince her. Maddie shook her head.

"I don't feel comfortable discussing my personal business at work," she told me.

"Fine," I said. I slid my hand down her arm and intertwined my fingers with hers. "Then we're leaving work."

"What's that supposed to mean?" she asked.

"I'm taking you to dinner. It looks like you've been forgetting to eat as well. Then you'll be out of the office and won't have to worry about the little bitch coffee machine anymore."

She grumbled a few protests, but it wasn't enough to actually stop me. I led her out of the office and down the street to a small diner. It was a gem hidden in plain sight.

It was simple but delicious, and I felt like it was the perfect place to share with Maddie. I got her inside, and she sagged in the booth. Sally, a sweet older waitress who always made sure I got extra hash browns, came up to the side of the table and smiled at me.

"Hey, there, Toby. How are you this evening?" she asked in a voice too dipped in honey to be originally from New York.

"Doing well, Sally. We'll both have some coffee," I replied, and she headed behind the counter.

A few moments later she returned with two mugs and menus tucked under her arm. She distributed them and walked away to tend to the other customers. I took a sip of coffee, then leaned on the table, my hands folded in front of me.

"All right. Here we are. No longer at work. So, go ahead. Tell me what's going on with you," I said.

Maddie was out of excuses, and she knew it. She took a sip of her coffee and let out a sigh.

"My little sister Megan has been acting out a lot lately, and it's making me worry," she said.

"Your little sister?" I asked. "I didn't know you had a sister."

She nodded. "I guess she's not actually so little. That's just how I still think of her. She's a senior in college now. She's always been a bit of a troublemaker. I hoped it would get better once she got in school and was heading down to the path toward adulthood. But it hasn't worked out that way. She's actually gotten wilder and is totally off track. Without me around to keep her in line, she hasn't been doing very well," she told me.

I looked at her strangely.

"What do you mean without you around to keep her in line? You've got your own shit together. Why would you be responsible for her?" I asked.

Maddie shook her head, looking almost defeated.

"It's just the way it's always been. My parents have always babied her. She could do no wrong in their eyes, and if she ever did do something wrong, it was my fault. I wasn't helping her with her homework enough, so she didn't get a high grade on a test. I wasn't there to support and encourage her, so she lined up with the wrong friends. It was always about me. Then I moved here, and that made it even worse. Now she guilt-trips me for not being in Kansas," she explained.

"That must be difficult, worrying about your sister," I said. It was obvious she really was concerned about her sister, but her downcast eyes and fidgeting told me there was something more to her agitation than that. "What else?"

"What do you mean?" she asked.

"Is there anything else bothering you? I'm not trying to pry, but you seem more upset than just someone worrying her younger sister might be having a girls-gone-wild moment," I said.

Sally showed up at the table again. We hadn't even ordered, but she had plates of food and set them in front of us.

"Tonight's special," she announced and walked away.

Maddie looked at me with a raised eyebrow, and I shrugged.

"I come here a lot. They know what I like," I explained.

She shook her head and reached for the ketchup to shake some onto the pile of crispy golden fries mounded up next to a massive burger.

"Rolling in money and eating at a greasy spoon. You're just full of surprises, aren't you?" she asked. She took a bite of a fry. "During our last phone call, Megan mentioned my ex would be coming up here soon to talk to me. It came across a little threatening."

"Threatening?"

She nodded. "Our relationship didn't end well, and Craig isn't the best guy. He is definitely one of the less than stellar decisions of my youth, and the effects of it are still lingering."

"What do you think he meant by he was coming up here to talk to you?" I asked.

I didn't like the way this sounded but tried to keep my emotions under control. I didn't know all the details of the situation and didn't want to escalate her any more by getting upset.

"Megan said he told her he would see me soon and has an important question to ask me. He was really unhappy when I broke up with him and didn't want to let me go. We went back and forth a lot during our relationship, and he didn't really believe it was over that last time. He might be coming to try and get me back." She drew in a breath and looked down at her lap for a second before lifting widened, glistening eyes to me. "I'm worried about what might happen when he gets here."

Protectiveness instantly rose up inside me. She hadn't given me all the information or explained why she was afraid, but she didn't have to. All that mattered was he frightened her, and she didn't want him around her. There was no way I was going to let her ex fuck with her. My hands clenched as I considered my options and how I was going to protect her.

CHAPTER 6

MADDIE

All the tension from the conversation with my sister and worrying about Craig's threatening message had built up until I felt like I was going to burst. My confrontation with the coffee machine didn't do much to calm me down. Finally letting it all out felt good, but it was a bit awkward to have it be Toby on the other side of the table. Spilling my guts out to him was weird, especially considering what had happened between us. It definitely toed the line of the professional relationship I insisted on us maintaining. An employee didn't generally pour her heart out and gush out all the struggles in her personal life to her boss.

But there wasn't anyone else I would even begin talking to about something like that. I missed Jane and wished she was there to talk to about what was going on. It was hard having her gone and encountering a situation like this without her made her absence stand out even more. It left me without any close friends in the city, and no one I could trust.

Except Toby. Even though he was my boss, he was dependable and steady. I knew I could count on him for discretion. It wasn't just that. If I was being totally honest, I knew there was an emotional element to sitting here opening myself up to him completely. I hadn't talked about it and had done everything I could to hide it, but I still had a huge crush on Toby. I liked being able to share something personal with him. Even if that personal story was fucked-up. It was especially difficult to talk about Craig. I hesitated to tell Toby about my ex and how much of an effect he had on my life even now so long after we broke up. Spilling about another man wasn't exactly something I dreamed of doing while sitting across the table from Toby. The twisted history of my love life wasn't ideal conversation for over a meal with him.

The strange reality of it aside, I was glad to be talking to Toby. I was frightened by the whole situation and saying it out loud helped to alleviate some of my anxiety. It was like sharing the reality of what I was going through took the edge off. If I was going through it by myself, it kept brewing and building, but telling Toby put it out into the world. It meant I wasn't dealing with it alone. It also felt like it gave me more perspective. Maybe I was just being foolish. Maybe Craig wasn't even coming to New York. It was probably just an idle threat he made because he enjoyed the game. It could be just an exercise of control, a reminder of his ability to manipulate me. That was something he always did extremely well when we were together. He was able to change my thoughts, my actions, and the way I saw the world around me at the drop of a hat. He got so good at it he could send me through wild shifts and changes in the course of a day at a whim, and for a long time I didn't even recognize what he was doing.

A big part of that manipulation was always creating fear and doubt in me. Fear of him, doubt there were any others in the world who would love or understand me. Fear of being alone, doubt I could survive any more time with him. There was always something, always a feeling in the back of my mind keeping me on edge. I was never really comfortable, never fully settled and at peace, not until I came to New York. Now he was just trying to do that again. The thought that Craig was just trying to create those feelings in me again and I was overreacting eased my tension a little more. I was just about to share the theory with Toby when he interrupted me. His words left me dumbfounded and blinking at him as I tried to force some semblance of thoughts through a mind left totally blank by his suggestion.

"Excuse me, what?" I asked.

"It would work. Seriously," he said.

I shook my head, rattling the words around in it until they came together in a cohesive thought.

"I'm sorry, I thought I heard you say marriage," I said.

"Fake marriage," he clarified. "Think about it. You're concerned about your ex coming to the city to try to win you back. You said the two of you went back and forth a lot in your relationship. That means you always took him back, right?"

I thought about all the horrible nights and the gushing apologies that followed. The times when I tumbled back into Craig's arms because I believed he would change and get better. Those eventually changed to taking him back because I didn't know anything else and had been broken down until I believed there wasn't anything else but him. Then it became out of fear of him. In the end, they weren't really any different. No matter what the motivation or how it happened, I ended up with him again, which put me right back in the position to be manipulated and abused until the next time I'd try to walk away. It was an awful cycle, but one I'd broken free of and was never going back.

"I'm not proud of it," I admitted. "But, yes."

"So, if he thinks you're still available, he could very well come here thinking the time apart has given you the chance to think things through and change your mind. He might try to woo you back, or worse, scare you back. But if he doesn't think you're available, there's less of a chance he'll bother you," Toby said.

"I don't think I'm following."

"If you're worried about your ex coming here trying to harass you and win you back, then there is one way you can make sure that doesn't happen. Show him there's no chance. If you're already married, then you don't have to worry about your ex pursuing you. He might be an ass, but guys like that want what they can have. He's not going to go through the effort of trying to take you away from a marriage," Toby said.

It was crazy. Absolutely batshit crazy. I leaned back against the booth and thought it through for a few seconds.

"Why jump straight to marriage? If I'm going to fake something, why not just have a fake boyfriend?" I asked.

Toby shook his head adamantly. "It's like I said, men like this guy want what's easy and accessible to them. He was your boyfriend once, so he knows someone being your boyfriend always has the potential of a breakup. With just a dating relationship, there's still a chance. If he showed up here and you told him you had a boyfriend, he would still be able to hang on to false hope. It has to be more serious than that. He has to see you've moved on with your life to the point that you're not just going to break up with a guy over an argument and be available to him again. It has to be a marriage."

"I mean, I guess that makes sense. I don't think Craig would be so obsessive he would go through the time and energy of convincing me to get a divorce. It would be too much effort for him, but it would also just be embarrassing. He'd never admit a woman good enough for him would purposely choose another man to marry. Me being married to someone else would be a flaw, and he'd just decide he never really wanted me to begin with," I said.

"Exactly. Saying you're not interested seems like you're playing hard to get. Presenting yourself as having a boyfriend is just a challenge and a chance for a conquest. Being married is the final straw. It's an easy, effective way to buck him and send him out of your life for good," Toby agreed.

I stared at him for a few seconds, then laughed.

"It's a great idea, but there's one serious chink in the plan," I pointed out.

"What's that?" he asked.

"I don't know anyone crazy enough to fake marry me," I told him.

That was the moment when I expected him to start laughing with me. We'd laugh it out, eat our delicious, terrible-for-us burgers, and go home feeling better. Then the next day I'd bring myself back into reality and start thinking about an actual way to handle the Craig situation. But Toby didn't laugh. Instead, he shook his head.

"You're wrong," he said. "I would."

The words seemed to bounce off me, not staying long enough for me to be completely sure I'd actually heard them accurately.

"What?" I asked.

"Me. I would marry you," he said.

That's what I thought he said, yet the shock wasn't any less. I couldn't believe what I was hearing.

"Why would you do that?" I asked.

He drew in a breath and reached across the table to take my hand in his.

"Because I care about you and want to keep you safe. If you're afraid of this man and think he might be capable of causing you any trouble when he comes to the city, then I want to be there for you. I can protect you from him," Toby explained.

I shook my head, only this time it was out of disbelief rather than trying to deny him.

"I'm probably overreacting. I'm sure Craig will turn out to be harmless. He might not even come to the city. He probably just wanted to have Megan tell me that so I'd know the two of them were in contact, which he knows I hate, and to make me worry because that amuses him."

Even as I said the words, I wasn't so sure. There were plenty of other opportunities for Craig to have Megan send me a message, and he'd never done something like this. In all the time I'd been in New York, he never even suggested he was going to come. Despite all my efforts to rationalize it to myself and talk myself down, this situation felt different.

"I'd rather be certain," Toby said.

He squeezed my hand, and I didn't pull away. My mind was spinning, and I didn't know what to think, much less how to respond. I couldn't believe he had even suggested something like that. Even more, I couldn't believe how much sense it made and that I was actually considering taking him up on the offer.

CHAPTER 7

TOBY

This plan was absolutely brilliant. I had to admit when I first heard Maddie describing the way her ex treated her and saw the fear in her eyes, my plans for how I was going to handle him weren't so magnanimous. Smashing him to pieces before he was able to set foot near her seemed like the best way to go about dealing with her worries. Then I thought about how that might affect her and realized more violence wasn't going to solve anything. At least, not as a first option. If there was a way to buck him off her and make it so he wasn't interested in sniffing around her anymore, it would be easier and far less messy for everyone involved.

That's when the idea of her pretending to be married came to mind. It was a stroke of genius, if I did say so myself. And not just for the most obvious reason. Faking being married to her meant I would get to protect Maddie and keep her out of the hands of that creep. But it also meant I would get to spend more time with her. Maybe, just maybe, all that extra time together and a little cozying up to each other for realism's sake would bring us closer so I would be able to convince her to try a real relationship. It sounded ideal to me, but I could immediately tell Maddie wasn't fully on board.

I wanted to convince her this was the perfect way to resolve the situation without causing too much drama and conflict. At the same time, I had to tread lightly. I didn't want to be too forceful and risk sounding like the very asshole ex she was trying to avoid in the first place. He'd spent the vast majority of their relationship manipulating her, and I didn't want to come across as doing the same thing. But I also wanted to be firm. Her safety was paramount.

"I know this sounds out there," I conceded. "But it's simple. Keeping you safe is the most important thing. If he thinks at all that he could get you back in his life, he's going to do everything he can to convince you to do it and that includes if he thinks you have a boyfriend. He'll just lay on the charm to lure you away. And if you don't respond, he'll see it as a rejection, and it could get nasty fast. Being married is different. You can't just drop everything and walk away from a marriage."

"It's nice of you to be concerned about me and come up with this plan, but I don't want to drag you into all this. You don't need to be involved in my drama and all wrapped up in my personal mess," she said.

"Maddie, listen to me. I care about you. I care about what happens to you, both physically and emotionally. I want to know you are safe and feel secure and comfortable. You're not asking me to do anything. You're not expecting anything from me. I am gladly offering you my protection," I told her.

Her expression changed just slightly. My rationale

seemed to be getting through to her. She laughed nervously, looking down at the table where I held her hand. Her eyes lifted back to mine, and she bit her bottom lip.

"If I'm really going to consider this idea, I need a drink," she said.

I grinned. "Then let's go get one."

Reluctantly taking my hand away from hers, I pulled out my billfold and tossed some money on the table to cover dinner and a nice tip for Sally. Maddie looked a little taken aback by my immediate and enthusiastic acceptance of her suggestion. I knew the location change was in part to break the rising tension between us, to force the conversation to break. She probably also saw it as an opportunity to laugh off my idea and try to reset us back to the point before I threw out the concept of us pretending to be married. I wasn't going to see it that way. I was treating this as an opportunity to convince her my idea was exactly the right thing.

Maddie let me help her out of the booth, and I touched my hand to the small of her back to guide her toward the door of the diner. Sally flashed me a smile as we walked out. I was sure that would lead to a lot of questions and probably some innuendo I wasn't necessarily comfortable with in the coming days, but it was worth it.

We walked across the street to the bar occupying the opposite corner and slipped onto two of the leather-cushioned stools. A bartender walked up to us, and Maddie ordered a glass of wine. I ordered bourbon, and when the bartender left to get our drinks, I turned to her.

"So? What do you think?" I asked.

"How would we make it seem realistic?" she asked.

"What do you mean?"

"We can't just say we're married and expect Craig to immediately believe it."

"All right. What do you think we need to seem convincing?" I asked.

"Where would we say we live?" she asked.

"My apartment, of course. It's much larger and in a more desirable part of town," I explained.

She made a face at me. "Thank you so much."

I laughed. "I only mean he would be suspicious if he thought you were married to someone wealthy but were still living in a small apartment."

"And what if Megan has already told him my address? She knows where I live. Maybe he'll just show up and start asking about me or see me there," she pointed out.

"All right. We say we've kept both apartments for now because our relationship is currently under wraps," I say.

The bartender brought our drinks, and Maddie quickly went to work taking hers down. I took a sip of the bourbon, and my mind went to Nik and his strange departure. We still didn't know exactly what was going on, but that was an issue to deal with later. Right now, I needed to concentrate on Maddie.

"Why would we be keeping it under wraps if we're married?" she asked.

"Because of the special circumstances of our professional relationship. It's still a delicate issue with work. Those who really need to know, do, but we haven't gotten so far as telling all the staff yet. We want to be careful and diplomatic about it so we're sure everyone handles it well and doesn't feel like something inappropriate is happening. We didn't have a big wedding, and we know it will come as a shock to many people, so we're just biding our time while we tell those closest to us and figure out how we're going to move forward," I said.

She nodded and finished her glass of wine. "That sounds very plausible. It also helps explain why Megan wouldn't have told him I was married. Maybe we just haven't gotten around to telling our family yet because we eloped and we're planning a ceremony. Or at least a reception."

"Exactly. We don't want to ruin the surprise or make them feel like they weren't involved, so we've only told the people who work closest to us so they aren't blindsided. Then we're going to make a big announcement and have a celebration with our family and friends," I agreed.

She nodded again and reached for the second glass of wine the bartender brought her. "How about our backstory?"

"What do you mean?"

"Everybody has a backstory, and it's the first thing people ask about when they find out someone is in a relationship they didn't know about, much less married. We need to have our details straight so it sounds like we're actually together," she explained. "How did we meet?"

"Work, obviously," he said. "You came to my company looking for a job in the big city. I was impressed by your resume and your interview, so I hired you. Then as we got to know each other, I was captivated."

It was the truth, and one day I hoped she would know that.

"And how did we fall in love? It couldn't have happened in the office because then everybody working there would know without us having to tell them. Water cooler gossip is real, and we don't even have a water cooler," she said.

I stared into her eyes. "It was on a business trip to Paris. We couldn't resist each other."

The heat and longing in my voice weren't lost on Maddie. She blushed and downed the rest of her wine. Lifting one hand, she gestured to the bartender for another glass. I was still sipping my way through the bourbon, pacing myself.

"What about our wedding?"

"Justice of the peace. We knew it was a sticky situation and would take some diplomacy and careful treading to handle with everyone around us. But we didn't want to wait to be married a second longer. We also knew people would expect a dramatic, lavish wedding, and neither of us were totally sold on that. The idea of an event like that is fine, but we wanted to be able to really enjoy each other and focus on being together on our wedding day rather than going through the motions of a big production. So, we had a private ceremony at the courthouse. That way we would be married and could deal with all the rest of the stuff as it came."

Maddie seemed impressed by the answer and nodded. She ordered another drink, and we kept talking, nailing down details about our relationship.

"What's your favorite ice cream?" she suddenly asked me after we decided she wouldn't wear an engagement ring because it would call too much attention.

"What?" I asked.

"Your favorite ice cream," she replied. "I would never be able to marry a man whose favorite ice cream I didn't know. It's a fundamental detail."

I laughed. "It is?"

"Yes. People who are married spend time watching TV together. They have colds and strep throat together. They stay up all night talking. All of that requires ice cream, which means we would know each other's favorite flavor. Mine is butter pecan," she told me.

"That is extremely well thought-out. Um. I guess if I had to pick a favorite, I would go with cherry chocolate chip. What about savory snacks? What's your favorite potato chip flavor?"

"Sour cream and onion. Sometimes layered with cheddar and sour cream. Which clearly illustrates why I have not been in a committed relationship since Craig," she joked.

"I don't know. That sounds delicious. And if we ate them together, it would balance each other out," I told her.

"Fair point," she said.

She finished off her wine, and we kept talking, exchanging details and preferences, chipping away at the distance between us under the guise of being able to pretend to be married. After several minutes she gestured to the bartender for another wine. I rested my hand on hers.

"Maybe you should call it a night," I told her.

She looked down into her glass like it was going to reveal all the secrets of the universe to her.

"That's probably a good idea. I'm almost convinced about this whole fake marriage thing," she said with a laugh.

"Come on," I said, getting down from my stool and reaching for her hand. "I'm going to escort you home."

"Oooh," she teased but took my hand. "Escort. Now you're getting fancy. You know that means we're going to have to balance it out by riding the subway back to my house."

"The subway? Why would we do that? I can just call my driver," I pointed out.

She scoffed. "Do you realize how ridiculous that sounds? Tell me something, Toby. Do you even remember a time in your life when you weren't able to just call your driver?"

I thought about the question and realized it was about much more than the subway.

"Point made. All right. Let's go," I said.

Maddie was still laughing at me by the time we were walking up to the door of her apartment.

"I swear, I wouldn't have been surprised if you pulled a tiny bottle of Lysol out of your pocket and started cleaning the seats," she said when she was able to catch her breath.

"It wasn't that bad," I argued.

"Don't pretend I didn't see you searching your pockets for a handkerchief or a tissue or something to sit on," she said.

"I wasn't going to sit on it," I told her. "I was going to use it as a makeshift surgical mask in case someone coughed at me."

She crumbled into laughter again, and this time I joined her. There was no way to argue I was out of my element in the subway. So accustomed to my driver and the three luxury cars I kept so I could decide what I wanted to ride on a whim, I'd apparently lost touch with public transportation. And just how very public it was.

"This is me," she said when we reached the door.

I didn't want the night to end. We were having too much fun together, and I wanted every moment of it to last. Just in case she slipped back away from me again and we lost the connection we'd built back up.

"Do you want me to come inside and check it out? Make sure no one is lurking around?" I offered.

She laughed but nodded. "Sure."

Maddie let me inside, and I made a dramatic show of poking around in the closets, jumping into each room, and scouring through drawers and cabinets. She followed behind me, giggling, and when I finished, she gave me a bright smile.

"Looks all clear to me," I announced.

"Thank you," she said.

She wrapped her arms around my neck, standing up on her toes to hug me. It was a sweet, friendly gesture, but the heat quickly grew. I nuzzled my face against the side of her neck and let my lips touch her soft skin. They brushed up to the curve of her jaw and across her cheek. Maddie turned her head, meeting me halfway in a soft kiss. That simple touch was enough to ignite the sexual tension between us, and we kissed again, deeper and more insistently.

We stumbled back a few steps through the living room. My goal was the hallway that led to her bedroom but going backward wasn't a particular strength for me. I miscalculated and hit the arm of the couch with the backs of my thighs. Feeling myself tumbling over backward, I grabbed onto Maddie and brought her with me. She laughed as we bounced on the cushions, and I held her tight, kissing her harder as I kicked off my shoes.

CHAPTER 8

MADDIE

Tangling my legs around Toby's, I held him close and kissed him deeper. His tongue dipped into my mouth, and I met it with mine. He lifted his head away from mine and looked down at me briefly before giving me a fast, hard kiss. I laughed as he buried his head in the side of my neck and nibbled at my skin. His hands touched the sides of my thighs and worked their way up until they tucked under my skirt. The groan in his throat when he found the tops my thigh-highs was enough to take the laugh right out of me. There was nothing funny about that groan. It was hot and insistent, telling me exactly what he was thinking without having to say a single word.

Toby pushed my skirt up to my waist and pulled back so he could look at the stretch of my thighs between the lacy top of the hose and my panties. I'd put the thigh-highs on that morning on a whim. Usually I wore regular pantyhose or had on slacks and didn't need them. But there was something about sliding on a pair of thigh-highs and lacy panties that made me feel stronger. Having a sexy little secret under my clothes, even when I had no intention of anyone else seeing it, took the edge off when I was feeling stressed and gave me more confidence. It didn't work enough that day to stop me from getting into a showdown with the coffee machine, but it was definitely having more than its intended effect on Toby.

His head dipped down, and his mouth found the tender inside of my thigh. An unexpectedly intense rush of sensation rippled along my skin and brought a burst of electricity to my core. He kissed the other thigh and brushed his lips up to the front of my panties. They were already damp, but his mouth closing over them brought another rush of arousal. His tongue slipped under the edge and slipped across as much of my sensitive tissue as it could reach before moving over to the other side.

I writhed against the couch, bringing my fingers to the buttons along the front of my blouse so I could open it. My skin tingled and ached with the need for more of his touch. I didn't want anything between us. Before I could take my shirt all the way off, Toby suddenly rose up and kissed along my stomach until it got to the swells of my breasts. He kissed each, sweeping his tongue along the edge of each cup like he was tracing the imprint of my lingerie onto my skin.

"We know so many details about each other now, and we came up with stories about our relationship. But we didn't decide on what our wedding night was like," he said in a lowered, almost conspiratorial tone. "I think we need some inspiration."

"Oh, do you?" I asked. He lifted his eyebrows at me, and I smiled. "I mean, if it's for realism purposes…"

Toby grinned and stood up. He scooped me off the couch and back over his shoulder. I squealed as he took off toward the bedroom. Tossing me onto the mattress, Toby paused at the end of the bed to shuck his clothes. I wriggled out of my shirt and reached behind me to lower the zipper on the back of my skirt. He took hold of it, and I lifted my hips so he could tug it off. Turning his attention back to my thigh-highs, Toby slowly peeled them off one at a time, kissing along the length of my leg as each inch of skin was exposed.

By the time he removed both and peeled my panties away, I had taken off my bra and was finally bare, open and ready for him. Rather than immediately coming down over me, Toby eased my legs apart and positioned himself between them. He settled his lips on the inside of one thigh again and started a trail of kisses up toward the ache of desire. This time, he didn't stop. The feeling of his tongue on me without the barrier of my panties made me cry out, and I gripped the blankets beside me. My eyes closed as I savored the decadence of his mouth exploring the most delicate, hidden crevices and recesses of my body. It moved across me with the same mastery as his fingers had the first time we were together.

That first night was still with me. I had wanted him since then, the desire and need never lessening even when I so steadfastly insisted there had to be nothing but professionalism between us. It worked for months. I managed to swallow down all my thoughts and feelings and keep them at bay as I leaned harder into my work. One day I wanted to be more than just the assistant director of the marketing department and keeping my focus sharp would get me there.

But all that resolve disappeared tonight. He was so sweet with me. When I poured my heart out to him, he didn't judge me or think differently. Instead, he tried to think of every way he could to protect and take care of me.

It broke down the guard I put up, and as soon as his lips touched mine, I knew I couldn't resist temptation anymore.

Fortunately, Toby was far from playing hard to get. His tongue worshipped my body and brought me to a delirious peak. Just as all the tension throughout my body shattered, Toby rose up over me and his hard cock plunged into me. The feeling sent me into another wave of pleasure. He didn't let up. There was nothing slow and experimental this time. He thrust into me hard and fast, groaning and hissing between his teeth as he drove deep. I pressed onto his chest and flipped him over onto his back so I landed on top, his shaft still buried within me. The new position gave me control, but I had no interest in slowing anything down.

Loving the way he watched me, I rolled my hips, grinding into him. Toby grabbed my hips with both hands, and his fingertips dug into my skin as he bounced me. His hips lifted to meet mine, and soon I crashed into another dizzying climax. The feeling of my body clamping down on his, seemed to push Toby over the edge, and he lifted his hips, slamming me down hard to impale me with a final thrust as he growled.

We were both gasping for breath when his hips dropped back down to the bed and I fell forward onto his chest. Our kiss was soft and gentle, a sweet, slow completion that guided our bodies to cool down and relax. Eventually I slipped to the side, so I settled beside him, and his arm looped around me to hold me close.

I couldn't remember the last time I'd felt so relaxed and contented, so completely satisfied and happy. Maybe never. The only thing that even came close to comparing to it was the last time Toby held me like this, but then the reality of Nik and Jane waiting for us back at the apartment hung heavily over us. We didn't have a chance to just relax together and enjoy basking in the afterglow in each other's arms. This night there was no such threat of discovery, no timetable put on us. I was able to just listen to the beat of his heart and let my body melt against his. Part of me knew I should probably get up. I should have rolled over, gotten dressed, and sent him on his way. But I couldn't. It felt too good to be right there in the warm crook of his body. I felt so safe and secure, and I couldn't help but let my eyes drift closed and have sleep overtake me.

It was just going to be a rest. I was just going to close my eyes and doze for a little while. But when I opened my eyes, I didn't see the darkness and shadows of my bedroom in the middle of the night. Instead, I was greeted by the hazy blue and purple sunlight of a somewhat foggy dawn. Realization settled in. It was morning. I'd fallen asleep in seconds and slept hard all night. There was none of the tossing and turning I usually did, none of the waking up and staring up at the ceiling. I was curled on my side with the blankets draped lightly over me. My body felt relaxed and calm, and I was refreshed rather than feeling groggy and reluctant like I usually did first thing in the morning.

Stretching luxuriously, I rolled over onto my back. My leg brushed against warmth beneath the covers, and I looked to the side. Toby was sleeping beside me, his hair tousled and his face peaceful. In that instant, it all crashed back down on me. I'd done it again. Holy hell.

As if he could hear my thoughts, Toby woke up and gave me a big smile from under his happily sleepy eyes.

"Good morning, beautiful," he said.

He opened his arms to me and rose up as if to give me a kiss, but I pressed my hand into the middle of his chest and eased him back.

"We can't keep doing this," I said.

"What do you mean?" he asked.

"If we're going to go through with our plan, we have to act professional. We have to avoid things like this," I told him. "We never should have let ourselves be alone together for as long as we were last night, and we definitely shouldn't have been drinking," I insisted.

"I wasn't drunk," Toby said. "And neither were you."

"I know that. I'm not trying to say we were. But... " I let out a sigh. "You know what I mean. This shouldn't happen."

"Is that really how you feel?" he asked.

"What do you mean?"

"You didn't seem to have a problem with it last night."

"I don't have a problem with it," I told him. "That's not what I mean. I'm not saying... Look. I'm attracted to you. I think that's very clear, but I'm also worried about my job. People aren't blind. What if someone noticed something? Or figured it out? I don't want to be known as the woman who slept with my boss to get ahead."

"But that's not what you did," he argued.

"I know. But that won't stop people from thinking it, and I love my job. I don't want it at risk."

Toby thought about this for a few seconds, then grinned again. "I guess we're just going to have to be discreet throughout our fake marriage."

I hesitated. "I don't know, Toby. I don't know if that's the best idea. I'm still on the fence." Toby got out of bed and moved around the room, finding his clothes. "I really appreciate you coming up with the idea and trying to protect me. But clearly, we aren't good at keeping things platonic and being in the same space without letting things go too far. I just feel like we're treading into sticky territory. We might be able to convince Craig he doesn't have a chance with me by faking being married, but what's all that time together really going to do to us? Are we going to be able to act like we're married and still keep enough distance so when he goes away we can go back to having a purely professional relationship?"

Toby finished getting dressed and walked up to the edge of the bed. He leaned forward and kissed my forehead.

"I need to go now, or you are going to be late for work," he said.

Without another word or waiting for me to respond, he walked out of the bedroom. A few seconds later, I heard the door close as he let himself out, leaving me sputtering in my bedroom, trying to figure out what exactly just happened.

My brain was still buzzing from the night before. I knew exactly what had happened. Every moment was etched into my memory, and I knew I would bring those moments forward again anytime I felt cold at night. Yet, I still couldn't completely believe what we'd done. Maddie was so insistent about us maintaining a completely professional relationship. She had even been hesitant to tell me what was bothering her. Discovering the heat still existed between us and she felt the same intense draw to me as I did to her was thrilling. I could see it in her eyes and feel it in the way she wrapped her arms around me. Nothing would stop me then. I just couldn't resist her. And I can't deny myself any longer.

The thoughts spinning around in my head and the spike of energy that came from spending the night with Maddie made it hard to keep myself focused that morning. I called my driver as soon as I left her apartment and started walking in the direction of my house. He picked me up along the way and brought me home so I could get into fresh work clothes. It seemed like a shame to shower away the smell of her, but I wasn't going to press my luck. I spent too long standing under the water thinking about Maddie, and by the time I got the office, I was already late, and that wasn't like me. Other than Nik, I was usually the first person there in the morning. I figured it was hard to run a company when things were happening before I was even there. Slipping into the front door felt awkward, like a teenager sneaking in past curfew after a night on the town. I half expected my assistant to be waiting for me, ready to chastise me.

But nothing happened. It was like no one had even realized I wasn't there. The receptionist at the front desk in the lobby was hunched over her phone, deep in a whispered conversation I was fairly certain had nothing to do with directing calls throughout the office. A cluster of people stood to the side, holding cups of coffee like props and leaning together to talk. One of them looked over at me, then leaned every closer and muttered something to his colleagues.

"Good morning, James," I called out so I could gauge his reaction.

His head broke out from the group again, and he lifted his coffee to me like he was giving me a toast.

"Morning."

That was it. My entire greeting from an employee I'd hired right out of school. What the hell was going on? I wondered what everyone was talking about, what was so fascinating. Then it hit me. Oh, shit. Was Maddie right? Had someone somehow figured out what had happened between us and was now spreading it through the office faster than a cold? The thought made my chest tight, thinking about how she would respond. The elevator doors opened, and three more people engrossed in conversation walked out. They passed right by me without even acknowledging me. In a way, that was reassuring. Surely if I was the source of salacious office gossip, I'd at least get a stare and maybe even a point.

I stepped into the elevator and hit the button for my floor. The doors were just closing when Ethan slipped through the gap. The move almost splashed the coffee right out of his hand, but he managed to save it. His grin was that of a man in the know.

"Good morning, Ethan," I said.

"Morning," he said.

"What is going on with everybody today? I'm late by an hour, and it's like I no longer have any idea what's happening," I said.

The director of my marketing department looked shocked. "Didn't you hear?"

"Obviously not."

"Nik is back," he said, "with Jane."

"With Jane?" I asked, surprised at that bit of news.

None of us had heard anything from Jane since she'd abruptly resigned. We didn't even know where she was or what was going on with her. Finding out she was back in the office wasn't what I expected, but it also didn't seem like quite enough to justify all the whispering.

"Yep. Apparently, she was in Paris all this time. And... incidentally... that's where they got married," Ethan said.

He just slipped that bit of information into the conversation casually, but it was in that casual way that sounded like he was going to burst at any second.

"Wait, what?" I asked.

That would definitely explain the upheaval in the office.

"Right?" Ethan said. "Shocked the hell out of me, too. But apparently, he went after her and they got married. Now they're back, and he's giving Jane her old job back."

He finished the story just in time for the elevator doors to open at my floor. Nik was standing just a few feet away down the hallway, and I patted him on his back.

"Hey, Toby. Good to see you," he said cheerfully.

"You, too. Can I have a word with you?" I asked.

He nodded and followed me to my office. I closed the door behind us and turned to him.

"Did you hear?" he asked.

"I did. Wow. I mean… how did all this happen? I didn't even know you and Jane had a relationship, much less that you were going to get married," I told him.

"To be honest, neither did I. Things were going on between us for a while, and after the business trip to Paris, I was sure I wanted to be with her. But that's when Angela showed up. I didn't handle the situation very well, and Jane ended up getting hurt," he explained.

"So, that's why she left," I said. I suddenly remembered something. "Wait… wasn't she engaged to someone else? There was that announcement in the paper."

"It wasn't really an engagement so much as a business arrangement. But Angela being here was only part of why she left. There was another factor at play," Nik said.

"What do you mean?" I asked.

"She's pregnant," he announced.

"Pregnant?" I asked, dumbfounded.

He smiled widely. "Yes. I found out when I got to Paris. Jane is having my baby. Soon."

"That's incredible. Congratulations."

"Thank you. I can't believe it's actually happening."

"I have to ask, though. What about the employee

conflict-of-interest policy?" I asked. "Is that going to cause trouble for the two of you since you're planning on giving her job back?"

He shook his head. "I'm not her direct supervisor. Technically if I don't make the final decision about her tenure or promotion, there's no conflict and we can smooth things over with HR as easily as coming up with some contracts. Putting things in writing is always a good workaround."

"That's fantastic news," I said.

I meant it for Nik and Jane, but it also paved the way for something more between Maddie and me. Now all I had to do was figure out how to approach her about the fake marriage. That morning made it very clear she wasn't convinced about the idea. The night before, she made it sound as if we only had to worry about it if her ex showed up. But by this morning she'd shifted to sounding like she believed the idea could never work. That was certainly a shame because I was hoping the arrangement would turn into many more nights like we'd had together. There was something about Maddie that got into my blood. I was already addicted to her and couldn't think about anything more than scooping her into my arms, carrying her back to bed, and burying myself in her all night long. It was making focusing on work more challenging, but I'd spent my entire adult life driving myself into the ground trying to get my software noticed and my company launched toward actual success. I could afford some time not pouring every ounce of myself into it. Maddie was well worth it.

Hearing about Nik and Jane and getting his explanation of how they would manage both their marriage and their professional life invigorated me. I didn't want to miss the opportunity, which I knew meant being careful. If I pushed too hard and came on too strong, it would scare Maddie away. I had to keep my hands to myself for now in order to convince her it could be an entirely fake marriage. We would do exactly what we planned, presenting ourselves as being married but keeping things under wraps. If this Craig dude showed up, I'd make it very clear that ship had sailed, and he could be on his way. Everything we learned about each other and the stories we wove would make it convincing. Hopefully not just to Craig, but to Maddie as well.

Pretending we were married and building up those feelings would be the perfect opportunity to get closer to her. Once I had her lured in, I could turn up my seduction game. Once she saw how good we could really be together, she would be ready to start something real.

But it wouldn't hurt to start doing some of the legwork. Telling stories and knowing each other's favorite foods was only going to get us but so far. We needed a backdrop, the real day-to-day stuff that made our shared life believable. Me not being at the office that morning was evidently barely noticeable to virtually everyone who worked there, so I figured it wouldn't cause much trouble if I just turned back around and went home. There was a lot to be done to make it look like we spent more time together than just when we were at work.

My new apartment was still a bit of a surprise when I walked inside. The money I made from the app made it possible to buy something much larger and more impressive than my last apartment. As big and expertly designed as it was, though, it looked decidedly like the home of a single man. I needed to figure out ways to make it look like she spent considerable time here. My first stop was the master bedroom. This seemed like the one place where it would be most obvious a married couple was sharing the space. We agreed to tell Craig she maintained her apartment, but it needed to look like she at least spent the majority of her time here and wasn't just living out of a duffel bag when she spent the night. It seemed foolish at first, since Maddie had never even been to my apartment, but I was ready to make her a permanent addition to my home and my life. By recreating the space for her, I could show her just how well she fit.

Grabbing my phone, I called the personal shopper I'd worked with to rebuild my wardrobe when my new level of success warranted a fresher look. I made a guess at Maddie's size, forwarded the shopper a picture of her to verify, and asked her to send over enough designer clothing to fill half my closet. From there, I connected with the home furnishings department and ordered several new decorative items I thought she might like. I needed to soften the room and make it look more like a space where a woman lived. The final thing I ordered was a new toothbrush. It seemed silly, but of everything I ordered, that was what made me smile the most. I couldn't wait until she used it for the first time after spending another night in my arms.

CHAPTER 10

MADDIE

I'd had days I thought were intense. I'd even had days I thought were crazy and would go down in the history of my life as standouts against all other days. This one topped them all. Starting from the very first moment I opened my eyes, the day was on a trajectory to be insane, and if I really wanted to get technical, it was crazy from even before that. If I could somehow pinpoint the moment when Toby first gathered me up and dragged me down with him as he fell onto the couch, it would likely show midnight found us being pretty ridiculous.

But I didn't even need to be that stringent about it. I would just start my tracking from the moment I woke up and Toby was sprawled out beside me that moment in of itself sent me reeling. It felt phenomenal, but I knew it couldn't last. And now, separated from that moment by several hours and a lot of other crazy things, there was a little voice in the back of my head asking, *Or can it?* Everything was suddenly different. My perception of the office, my job, and trying to fit Toby into the context of it all had taken a major shift the moment I looked up and saw Jane walking back into the office.

Her showing up on Nik's arm, and showing a nearly full-term pregnancy as well, might just change everything. Them being together didn't shock me nearly as much as it did some of the other people in the office. I had noticed the way they looked at each other as soon as he met her, and she quickly fell right into line with it. The two of them had a magnetic pull, and I knew eventually it was going to yank them right into each other's arms. I had an inkling something had happened between them when we were on our trip to Paris. Her very round belly proved it was much more than just a suspicion. I was dying to talk to her about it and find out everything. We had six months to catch up on, and I couldn't wait to get in some good girl talk.

We finally made it to the end of the workday, and I hurried up to her before Nik could scoop her away. He had that look the husbands of pregnant women get. Somewhere in that blonde billionaire head of his was images of tucking her away in a recliner and insisting on the world revolving around her. It didn't sound like torture, but I needed to get some time with her before all that started.

"Come on, let's go out," I said. "I've missed you so much."

"Yes!" she said excitedly. "I've missed you, too. We have a lot to talk about."

I laughed. "I see that."

"Where are you going?" Nik asked, coming up behind her.

"We're just going to go grab a couple of drinks like old times," I told him, looping my arm through Jane's.

It was meant to be a gesture of affection, but it likely came off looking more like I was aligning myself for a protest. I'd create a human chain to prevent her from slipping off into marital bliss and not hanging out with me.

"Drinks?" he asked, his eyebrow and his voice raising at the same time.

Jane sighed and rested her free hand on his chest.

"Shirley Temple all the way," she said. "And we'll split some appetizers. I promise, this Happy Hour will be pure Snacky Hour for me."

He was still grumbling about it, but Jane rose up on her toes to give him a kiss, and we scurried out. Having drinks after work with Jane used to be one of my favorite things before she left. It didn't take long being in our favorite bar for me to remember how much fun we always had together.

"All right, you've got to explain all this to me," I said, gesturing to her belly and the ring on her hand. "Because you seriously just up and disappeared. You were gone for six months without a single word."

She cringed and ate a handful of nuts from the bowl the bartender put between us when we sat down.

"I know. I'm so sorry about that. I should have said something or given you a better explanation than just the resignation letter. There was just so much going on, I didn't know what to say or how to say it," she said.

"So, explain it now," I suggested.

"Do you remember when Nik's ex-wife showed up?" she asked.

I rolled my eyes and reached for some of the nuts.

"How could I forget? That ice queen's ass made the office cold for a month," I said.

Jane laughed. "Definitely. Well, Nik and I were just starting to talk about the possibility of being a couple. I wasn't sure about the dynamics and I was worried about what it would mean for my professional life, but I was also falling so hard for him. Then she showed up and everything seemed to change. He wasn't paying attention to me anymore; he didn't try to talk to me about us. Then I found out I was pregnant. A little souvenir from Paris. I was so confused and upset. I thought Nik and his ex-wife were back together, and there was no way I was going to be that pathetic girl from the office who got knocked up and thought it would trap him. So, when the man my parents wanted me to agree to marry offered an engagement to get our parents off our backs, I saw it as my way out. Agreeing to marry Preston meant I got access to my family's money again, I would be able to go back to Paris, and I could just figure out life from there."

"But why didn't you tell anybody? Even me?"

"I didn't want it to get back to Nik. I was looking at a life by myself, so I figured I needed to start that right from the beginning."

"How did Nik find out about the baby?" I asked.

She laughed and shifted out of the way so a waitress could put down the plates of appetizers we'd ordered. Jane immediately dove in, running her hand along her belly as she delved into the pile of potato skins.

"He showed up in Paris," she told me. "My parents put that engagement announcement in the newspaper, and he saw it."

One hand covered my mouth for a second. "I know when that happened. Ethan and I were looking at it and Nik came in. He was pissed. He snatched the newspaper and left."

She nodded. "Well, apparently he left and basically went right to the airport. He showed up in Paris and saw my belly when I walked up to him. He thought the baby was Preston's and was really upset about it. But after I explained, it was so wonderful. He proposed to me right then. He said he should have asked me to marry him the first night we were together, before we even went to Paris. He knew he wanted to be with me and didn't want to wait any longer. We got married in a private ceremony right in the city before coming back to New York."

Jane looked dreamy as she finished the story, and I felt a little twinge in my heart even through the happiness for my friend.

"That is so romantic. I'm so happy for the two of you. And even more that you're back," I told her.

"I am, too. I love Paris, but it's not home. I really missed you, Maddie. Especially during those six months I spent alone in Paris. So, you've heard the whole saga of my growing life. Now, tell me what's been going on with you."

She reached into the basket of onion rings and ate a few as she stared at me with expectation. I drew in a breath and let it all out. She listened in shocked silence, working her way through the snacks as I spilled everything about my sister, Craig, and then Toby. When I was finally finished, I sagged with one arm against the bar and downed my drink. It might be a Snacky Hour for Jane, but I was still looking for the Happy. She gave me a grin, a bit of a twinkle in her eye.

"I thought there was something up between the two of you on our business trip," she said.

I nodded. "The last night when we left you and Nik at the café, we had a one-night fling. But we agreed right from the start that was it. Just one night. And it was going fine. We've been good at work, pretending Paris never happened. It was going right according to plan. Up until last night."

"What happened last night?" Jane asked.

I told her about the phone call with my sister and how it

led to the argument with the coffee machine Toby rescued me from before bringing me to dinner.

"I finally told him everything about my ex, and he suggested a fake marriage to throw Craig off so he wouldn't harass me if he actually did end up in the city. Then he brought me back to my apartment, and he searched it for me to make sure no one was there. It was just so sweet and funny, and I just couldn't take it anymore. All those months of trying to resist him built up, and we ended up spending the night together," I admitted.

"We'll hold that aside for just a second. I'm still back at him suggesting the fake marriage," Jane said. "What does that mean, exactly? You just pretend to be married so he won't keep pursuing you?"

"Basically, yes."

"Who are you supposed to be married to? Wouldn't your ex notice if you were talking about a husband, but one never materialized?" Jane asked.

"Well, that's the thing. He suggested I marry *him*."

Jane looked surprised. She sat back and looked at me for a few seconds.

"How do you feel about that?" she asked. "What do you think of the idea?"

"I'm not sure what to think," I told her. "It seems like a good idea in theory, but it all comes back to Toby. I'm afraid getting too close to him could be just as dangerous as seeing Craig alone. Just for very different reasons."

Spending time with Jane made me feel much better, even if she wouldn't tell me what she thought of the situation or what I should do. It was nice to just talk to her again and to share everything that was going on. But my good feelings didn't last. As I walked up to my apartment building that night, I came face-to-face with Craig who was waiting right outside.

My stomach turned and my heart immediately started racing in my chest as worry rushed through me.

"What are you doing here, Craig?" I asked.

"We need to talk," he said, taking a few steps toward me. "Let's go up to your place."

I shook my head.

"No. I don't feel comfortable inviting you into my apartment alone," I told him.

"Why?" Craig asked. "We've been alone together plenty of times before."

I floundered, stuttering and stumbling over my words as I tried to come up with something that wouldn't sound like I was afraid of him. I was tired of him having the power over me, knowing he could create fear in me. Finally, there was nothing I could do.

"Things have changed," I blurted out. "I'm a married woman now, and it's not appropriate to have another man in my apartment."

Well, here we go, I thought to myself. *No turning back now.*

Craig's eyes widened, but he didn't walk away.

"I'm surprised to hear you say you're married. Especially since no one, including your little sister, has mentioned it," he said.

"We haven't announced it publicly yet," I told him.

"Fine," he said with a smile that made a slimy shiver go down my back. "Then let's go to a coffee shop and talk. There'll be plenty of people around."

Afraid of screwing the situation up even more, I shook my head.

"I can't tonight. I'm running late from work, and I need to get home. I have dinner plans with my husband."

Craig was visibly annoyed. His shoulders straightened, and he leaned his neck back and forth as if to loosen stiffened muscles.

"No problem, I'll drop by your office tomorrow to take you out to lunch."

CHAPTER 11

TOBY

One of the most important things I had learned about success in the time I'd been working with Nik was to never let up. The success of the app was fantastic, but I couldn't let myself get complacent and think it would just continue to ride that way. I needed to keep pushing, never letting myself sit still. The first campaign was amazing, but now we had to top it. We had to come up with something even more compelling to make sure this wasn't our peak.

To make sure we were on the right track, I headed for the marketing department to check in with Ethan. The day before, he'd given me an early report on the next campaign and said he had more to show me. As I walked toward his office, I couldn't help but glance over at Maddie's. The glass panels to either side of the door gave a direct view into the room, and I expected to see her sitting at her desk, deeply invested in her work. Instead, she was pacing back and forth, chewing on her thumbnail. That wasn't like her, and I was immediately worried.

I knocked on the door, and when she opened it, I was

even more concerned. Her eyes were bloodshot like she hadn't gotten much sleep, and her face was pale and drawn. Something had deeply upset her.

"What's wrong?" I asked.

She gestured for me to come inside, and I stepped closer, closing the door behind me. I wanted to reach out and take her into my arms for a reassuring hug but didn't. After everything she'd expressed to me yesterday, I didn't want to go too far. She paced back and forth for another few seconds before stopping in front of me and looking into my face.

"Craig was lurking around my apartment building last night," she said.

"Craig, your ex?" I asked. "He's here in the city?"

"Yes. He was there when I got back. He tried to get inside, saying we needed to talk."

"Did you let him in?" I asked.

She shook her head hard and started pacing again.

"Of course not. I told him I couldn't talk to him right then. But he said he's coming here today to take me to lunch."

My hands clenched by my sides, and anger surged up into my face. I hated that I wasn't there. Maddie and I had no way of knowing he was going to be in the city this soon, and it infuriated me that he'd surprised her, and I wasn't there to protect her. Whatever it took, I was going to make sure I never made that mistake again.

"What did you do? What did you say to him?" I asked.

She sagged slightly like she didn't want to admit what was coming next.

"When I saw him standing there, I panicked. I figured if he actually was going to come to the city, I would have some sort of warning. More than just my sister telling me he was coming. I figured he would call me or something. Not just show up at my apartment. Then he told me we needed to talk, and he wanted to come inside. I had to do something. I needed to stop him from getting into my apartment because there was no way I wanted to be alone with him. I was scrambling for an excuse, trying to come up with anything that would send him away with as little conflict as possible." She drew in a breath and let it out. "So, I told him I was married."

I shouldn't have been happy to hear that. She was afraid and overwhelmed, and using the excuse of the fake marriage was a last resort. But I was glad it was there for her. If she had encountered him without any sort of explanation or emergency plan to fall back on, I didn't know what she would have done. At least this way, our plan was in action and we had some sort of idea how to move forward. She wasn't just floundering by herself. I was there with her.

I stepped up closer to Maddie, taking her by her upper arms to stop her pacing. She kept her focus away from me, like she was embarrassed about what she'd done.

"Hey. Look at me," I said. She reluctantly turned her eyes to me, and I could see tears starting to form in them. "You did the right thing. You made exactly the right choice. This was what we planned. And it worked. You told him you were married, and he left you alone. Just exactly the way we wanted it to happen. I'm sorry he scared you and that you were alone the first time you saw him. But I'm really glad you trust me to help you," I told her.

"Well it only halfway worked," she said.

"What do you mean?"

"I told you, he said he was coming here today to take me to lunch so we can talk. Telling him I'm married obviously didn't scare him off completely," she pointed out.

"Maybe not immediately, but it was a start. And if he insists on coming here and trying to talk to you, then he's going to have to come face-to-face with your husband," I told her.

"What do you mean?" she asked, looking suspicious.

"We're going to keep this story up. Just telling him you're married and talking about your husband might not be enough for this guy. But he's not going to be able to work around it if he has to see it. I'm going to go to lunch with you as your husband. After all, it wouldn't be appropriate for a man to bring a married woman out to lunch by himself. Especially a man with a romantic history with that woman," I said.

Maddie didn't look sure. She shifted her weight back and forth.

"I don't know if that's a good idea," she said.

"Why not?" I asked.

"We just came up with the stories about our relationship. What if we can't keep it up?"

"We will. It's going to be fine. It's lunch, not an interview. Think of it this way... men like I'm assuming your ex is, love to talk about themselves. They can't imagine a more important topic of conversation. If he starts asking us questions and we don't feel like we can maintain the story well, we turn the conversation over to him. We ask him about himself and get him to talk." I took her hands in mine. "This is going to work out. And I will feel much better if I don't have to think you're out there with him by yourself."

Finally, Maddie agreed, and I left her office for Ethan's. I paid close attention to the clock, not wanting Craig to get even a second alone with Maddie. I stood right outside her office with her. It gave us a direct view of the elevator and ensured the first time he saw her, he had to see me, too. It was almost one when the elevator doors opened, and a man stepped through. Maddie tightened beside me.

"That's him," she whispered.

I strode toward him, cutting off his progress before he was able to make it much farther into the office.

"You must be Craig," I said, extending my hand toward him. "I'm Toby, Maddie's husband."

He shook my hand, and it was all I could do to resist crushing every bone in it right there. The animosity between us was palpable, but it went beyond just jealousy over Maddie. I couldn't stand the man from the instant I laid eyes on him. Tall and muscular with a swagger that said he thought he was far more important than he actually was, he reminded me of the jocks in high school. The jocks who used to pick on me and push me around for being a skinny nerd. Since then I'd filled out and made close acquaintance with the gym, so I stayed fit and strong, but it didn't completely take away those memories. Back then I was defenseless, and assholes like Craig were happy to torment me in the halls every day, but not anymore. Now I was a force to be reckoned with.

Craig was a decade removed from high school, but it didn't seem like he had gotten over that persona. He was the same arrogant bully, and I could instantly see what Maddie told me about him. She came up behind him, and I glanced down at her. It was clear she was uncomfortable with the whole situation.

"Come on," she said. "We should go to lunch."

She wanted us out of the office as fast as she could and rushed us around the corner to a tiny, quiet restaurant. It was a place I'd walked past before but had never gone inside. A Middle Eastern deli with only a small handful of tables, it was somewhere she obviously hoped no one from work would come to and stumble on the confrontation.

As uncomfortable as the initial contact was, lunch was another level of awkward. We sat at the table in the back corner of the restaurant with Maddie and I squeezed together on one side of the booth. She kept her hands in her lap, and I could feel her picking and twisting at her fingers in the way she did when she was anxious. Craig was making her nervous, and the longer it took for the conversation to get going, the longer it was going to be before we could get this over with. I decided to take over.

"So, Craig. What brings you to New York?" I asked.

He didn't even look at me. Instead, he leaned across the table toward Maddie and began peppering her with questions.

"When did you get married?" he demanded. "No one has heard about it. Not even your sister."

"Not too long ago," Maddie said. "Just a couple of months."

"How did you meet this guy?" he asked as soon as the words were out of her mouth.

"We work together, obviously," she said.

"I guess you figured just banging the boss wasn't going to give you enough of a leg up in the office? You had to marry him, too?" Craig asked.

"That's enough," I said, stepping in. I wasn't going to let Maddie get bullied by this guy. "Our relationship is nothing like that, not that it's any of your business. No one at the office knows about our marriage. We agreed before we got married, we were going to keep it quiet at work until the right time."

Craig immediately pounced on that announcement.

"That's very convenient. You get to have all the perks of

being married to her, but none of the responsibility. Maybe big Mr. Bossman is afraid of a harassment lawsuit?" he asked in a mocking tone that made me want to punch the grin off his face.

But it was Maddie who jumped in this time. She was obviously tired of his needling and wanted to end this now.

"What are you doing in New York, Craig?" she asked firmly. "What do you want? Because if it's just to insult my new husband, you can waltz right back to your car and go back to Kansas right now."

"I flew," he said as if that made a tremendous difference to the situation.

"I don't care if clicked your heels together three times. I'm not going to sit here and let you insult my husband or me," she said.

I was proud of her, enjoying the spark showing up inside her. But the slow, feral smile that slithered its way onto Craig's lips dampened the spirit.

"Don't flatter yourself," he said. "The insults are just a perk. The real reason I'm here is to get your blessing."

"My blessing?" Maddie asked, her expression confused.

"I'm going to marry Megan."

CHAPTER 12

Bright sparks of light burst in front of my eyes, and ringing in my ears drowned out everything else around me. I felt like my head had just exploded. There was no way I'd heard Craig correctly. He couldn't have I said what I thought he just did.

"Megan? Like my little sister Megan?" I asked. "You seriously think you're going to marry my little sister?"

It had to be a joke. A seriously fucked-up joke he was pulling just to piss me off and make me miserable. It was the only explanation. I was furious, but I couldn't help the laugh that bubbled up out of my throat. It ached in my cheeks, then burst out of me. It was a completely ridiculous reaction, but it wouldn't stop. I laughed hysterically, so hard my stomach hurt, and tears stung in my eyes.

This was absurd. Craig coming in here and trying to hurt me by saying he was going to marry my sister was ridiculous. When I finally calmed down enough to look at Craig again, I saw the smug smile on his face. He was leaned back in the booth, relaxed and unaffected as he watched me. There was no hint of anger or an attempt to get under my skin. Out of the corner of my eye, I saw Toby look back and forth between us. He looked confused, like he felt like he missed something.

"You seriously came all the way from Kansas and accosted Maddie at her house just for that? You came all this way just to tell her you're marrying her sister?" he asked. "I call absolute bullshit on that. Why not a phone call? You had Megan call Maddie to tell her you were coming to New York and had something important to ask her, but you couldn't just pick up the phone and call her yourself? And speaking of Megan, if it was so important for you to get Maddie's blessing, why didn't you bring Megan along with you?"

My laughter disappeared, and it was replaced by anger as Toby fired off his barrage of questions. It caught Craig off guard, and the smile faded from his face.

"You sat right there and made a huge deal out of no one knowing about Maddie's and my marriage, but obviously Maddie had no idea you and Megan were even involved. Was your entire intention to be a hypocrite and act like an ass, or was that just another of the 'perks?' When did you start dating Megan? Why didn't either of you mention it to Maddie? When did you get engaged? When are you planning on getting married?" Toby continued.

Craig's face got red. It was obvious he was getting angrier by the second. This apparently wasn't how he envisioned this announcement going. He stood up, glaring at both Toby and me.

"I didn't expect an interrogation," he said through gritted teeth.

"What *did* you expect?" I asked. "You thought you could just come here and tell me you're marrying my little sister and I'd be fine with it? I'd jump for joy and clap my hands and tell you how wonderful I thought this whole bullshit plan is? Maybe I'd throw my arms around you and welcome you to the family and tell you I just can't wait to have you as my brother?"

"I did this as a courtesy," he said.

"A courtesy?" I asked incredulously. "You've got to be fucking kidding me."

"I see living in New York has done wonders for your class and sophistication," he snapped.

"Says the man with a tattoo on his ass that says, 'Get in Line' because he got so drunk at a frat party he didn't know what was happening," I replied.

"Look, I came here to tell you myself because I thought it was the right thing to do. Considering our history, I thought it might cause some problems and wanted to clear the air. But I don't need your permission. I'll marry Megan regardless of how you feel about it," Craig said.

That brought me right to my feet and sharply up in front of him. I glared at him, wanting him to look directly into my eyes and see I wasn't wavering.

"You will keep away from my sister if you know what's good for you," I growled at him.

Craig smiled down at me. The look was evil, taunting. He knew exactly what he was doing, and it only made me angrier.

"Are you threatening me, Maddie?" he asked.

There was an underlying message there, a hidden meaning to the words that he knew I'd catch. It was a reminder of everything he put me through and just how much he was capable of. I had no doubt the time apart only made him stronger and more vindictive. In those simple words he was telling me to watch myself, that I still had every reason to be afraid of him even if we weren't together.

Toby stood up beside me and wrapped an arm around my shoulders. He pulled me in close so I could feel the warmth of his body and the strength and steadiness of his muscles. I breathed in the smell of him, trying to calm myself down. I didn't want Craig to see me shaking, to know just how much he had gotten to me.

"There's no need to threaten anyone," he said. "Clearly we all need some time to calm down."

He had been reassuring and comforting, but that statement pushed me right back into my anger. I pulled away from Toby and stepped up closer to Craig. I was within inches of his face, close enough that the tips of my shoes were touching his, and each of my ragged breaths made my stomach brush against his. I needed to be that close. I needed him to see I wasn't going to wither away from him and try to hide behind Toby. Sticking a finger into the middle of his chest, I stared intensely into his eyes.

"Stay the fuck away from my little sister," I said through gritted teeth.

Turning on my heel, I stormed out of the restaurant.

Getting out of the small, dimly lit deli and back out into the fresh air helped to cool the burning of my cheeks, but it did little to calm me down. I stomped away from the restaurant, not even paying attention to where I was going. I didn't know which direction I turned after leaving or if I was headed back toward the office or not. It didn't matter. I just had to get out of there. I had to get away from Craig. A second longer of looking at his face would have done me in.

I was so furious I could barely see straight. Nothing around me was registering. All I could think about was Craig and the sickening thought of Megan latching herself to him. Suddenly, I heard footsteps pounding toward me. For a brief moment I thought it might be Craig and readied myself to launch into him again. But when I turned to look over my shoulder, I saw it was Toby, running to find me. His expression was tense and concerned. I paused and let him catch up to me.

"Maddie," he called out to me as he slowed and jogged the last several feet to me. "What are you doing? You aren't even going the direction of the office."

I threw my arms up in the air.

"So what? I don't care where I'm going," I told him.

Toby took my hand and pulled me over to a nearby bench in the shade of a large tree. Being out of the sunlight took some of the sting out of my eyes and helped me to focus, but it did nothing to calm me down. Toby sat and yanked me down onto the seat, turning me so I had to face him.

"Obviously, lunch didn't go well," he said.

"You think?" I snapped sarcastically.

He didn't let the attitude get to him. He stayed calm and held my hand gently in his.

"It could have gone a lot better, but it's a good thing your husband has your back," he said.

He grinned at me, but I just glared back.

"It's a good thing you had my back?" I asked. "How exactly is that a good thing? Did you stop him from announcing he's marrying my little sister? Did you convince him to go home and end things with her?"

"No, but I also didn't flip the fuck out, which is what you're currently doing," he pointed out.

The bluntness startled me off the edge, and I took a breath.

"You're right. I'm sorry. I shouldn't talk to you like that.

You didn't do this. I'm just... I don't know what to do," I said.

"Which, again, is why I have your back. We're going to think through this calmly and realistically. Clearly you were surprised to hear he's planning to marry your sister. You had no inkling at all that Megan was seeing Craig?" he asked.

I shook my head. "None. I've always told Megan to stay away from him. As soon as he and I broke up, I told her she needed to steer clear of him." I let out a sigh, glancing down at my thighs and then Toby's hand holding mine before looking into his face again. "There's something I didn't tell you. When you asked me why my approval means so much to Megan and why I'm the one who has to be responsible for her, I didn't tell you it's just the two of us. Our parents died when I was younger."

Toby looked stunned.

"I'm so sorry. I had no idea. You talked about them like they were still alive. I just figured..."

"I know. I really don't like to talk about it. It's still really hard even though it's been a long time. Sometimes it's just easier to not tell people and to keep them in the back of my mind, like they are still around, just off some-where where I can't see them," I explained. "But that's why I'm so protective of her. I've always had to be. It's true that my parents always favored her and did every-thing for her. She got used to that. What I told you about them was the way it really was. They really did expect me to always help her and be there for her. I was the older sister, so I was supposed to be the example and the one who did everything right so Megan would follow in my footsteps. It's almost like they knew somehow. Like they could predict there would be a time in the not too distant future when they wouldn't be around anymore, and I would have to be the one who was there to take care of both of us."

"I'm so sorry," Toby said again. "You know, you did tell me Megan has been acting out a lot recently. Maybe this is just one of the ways she's acting out?"

I nodded, feeling numb. This couldn't be happening. I couldn't force the reality into my brain. It wouldn't accept it.

"Maybe," I finally whispered.

Toby stood and gently pulled me to my feet.

"You should take the rest of the day off work," he suggested. "You're in no state to go back to the office. Everything will be fine there without you for one day."

I nodded and let him lead me to a cab. I climbed in and he followed, sitting close beside me and taking my hand again.

"Where are we going?" I asked.

"You'll see. I think you need a quiet space to relax and get a hold of yourself again," he told me.

CHAPTER 13

I held Maddie's hand while we were in the cab, wanting to stay as close to her as possible and maintain a connection with her during the drive. We weren't going to be in the cab for long, but even a few seconds felt like too much to not be near her. Especially with what she was going through. Maddie had proven herself unpredictable. Her reaction to Craig at lunch worried me. Not that she had ever been a shrinking violet before. She was bold and opinionated, and always made sure her thoughts were known. I couldn't imagine her to be the type of person to let others walk on her. But I had never seen her openly hostile before. She was far more likely to be the one mediating an argument and walking both sides through the situation to an eventual agreement. Not threatening a physical confrontation with someone.

This situation with her ex was clearly going to be far more complex to navigate than I originally anticipated. When I'd just thought he was an obsessive ex wanting to show up and attempt to draw her back into a relationship, it seemed straightforward. All we had to do was convince him she was completely and permanently off the market, and the thought of having to put forth so much effort would make him lose interest. He would leave her alone, and she wouldn't have to deal with him anymore. Now it wasn't so simple. Her assumption that the big question he had to ask her had to do with their relationship was out the window. I didn't understand how he could even begin to think that marrying her younger sister was a decent thing to do. On the other hand, from everything Maddie had told me, the fact that it was completely outlandish and inappropriate might have been a significant motivating factor for all of it.

She was struggling with the entire idea. I was going to do everything I could to support her and keep her from getting hurt, but even considering Megan marrying him was a major curveball. It put her in a state of mind I'd never seen Maddie in before. She was angry, but also seemed overwhelmed and even a little frightened. It was like there were so many emotions going on inside her she didn't know which one to follow or where to go.

The cab pulled up to the address I gave the driver, and I paid him before climbing out. I walked around to Maddie's door and opened it. She looked up, blinking at the towering apartment building as I helped her out of the cab. Holding one hand over her eyes, she leaned back to take in the entire height of the building.

"Where are we?" she asked.

"I'm bringing you to my place," I told her.

"Your place?" she asked.

"Yes. I told you I thought you should go somewhere quiet where you could relax and have a chance to think through everything," I told her. "This is the perfect place."

"Why couldn't I just go home?" she asked. "Nobody lives with me. It would be quiet there."

I took her hand and guided her into the building.

"Craig knows where you live," I pointed out. "Remember, he just showed up at your building yesterday? What's to say he won't do that again? And maybe this time he won't be as understanding about not going upstairs with you if he asked to. This is safer, and you have a better chance of being able to relax here. And when you're ready, we can talk this whole situation out and figure out what we're going to do next."

Maddie didn't seem thrilled at the prospect of me bringing her to my apartment without telling her, but she didn't resist when the doorman opened the front door to the building, and I guided her through. We crossed the small lobby and went to the elevator. The doors opened and we stepped inside the mirrored cubicle. She looked impressed when I took out my key and used it in the panel beside the keypad. That key allowed the elevator to rise up to the private floors at the top of the building taken up by my apartment. I brought her inside and didn't say anything as she looked around.

The space was large and airy, full of natural light from the massive windows on either side. The professional decorator I'd hired as soon as I'd bought the place made it tasteful and attractive, if slightly generic.

"I'm still looking for a few ways to make it more me," I told her.

I wasn't sure exactly why I had the compulsion to tell her that. It was almost like I was reassuring her. Like I wanted to make sure she saw the apartment as versatile and adaptable, a place she could settle into. Maddie nodded and walked over to the wall of windows to one side of the main room. She stood close to the glass and looked out over the park nearby. I walked up beside her, and we gazed out over the lush green oasis in the middle of the city.

"This place must have cost a pretty penny," she said.

It wasn't a question or even a condemnation. It was just an observation. A clean, straightforward acknowledgement. This was much more like Maddie, but it didn't make me any less on edge. I shrugged, slightly embarrassed by my surroundings. I loved my apartment and was proud of what I'd achieved, but the sudden enormity of my newfound wealth was still strange to me. I wasn't yet completely used to the seemingly endless money and tremendous luxury it could afford, but having Maddie there made it seem far less strange. Her being with me made me feel less out of place in the apartment, like she filled a space that helped me settle in more. This was the type of home I wanted to be able to give to her. The type she deserved.

I took her hand and led her through the living room and into my bedroom. We walked through the large cream-colored double doors at the back and went into my in-suite bathroom.

Leaving her in the center of the room, I went to the linen closet to gather freshly washed and dried towels. I stacked them on the counter and gestured to the large soaking tub at the side of the room. She looked at me quizzically.

"You should take a bath," I told her. "Try to relax. The warm water will help."

Maddie looked at me like I was crazy, but I wasn't going to take no for an answer. She was tense and anxious, and I wanted to help her feel better. She didn't move out of the middle of the floor, so I walked past her to the tub and turned the faucet handles so it started to fill. I tested the water on the inside of my wrist to make sure it wasn't too hot but would be warm enough to release the tightness in her muscles and soothe her.

When I first moved in, my real estate agent left me various gifts throughout the apartment to welcome me and help me settle in. One was an overflowing basket of bath products sitting on the counter between the dual sinks. I'd stuffed everything into cabinets and drawers, where they stayed until right then. Taking out several bottles of fragranced oils and bubbles, I drizzled them into the water. The surface covered in a creamy froth and piles of bubbles while the air filled with fresh, sweet scents.

I went into the bedroom and opened my closet. The clothes the personal shopper had bought looked great hanging there beside mine. I pulled out the plush robe she'd selected along with the other garments and brought it into the bathroom. Maddie looked at it as I hung it on the hook on the back of the door. One hand lifted almost limply to point at it.

"Is that in my size?" she asked.

I nodded. "Yes. Now, go ahead and relax. I'm just going to call the office and let them know we're not going to be back in for the day. That way no one expects us and won't bother us." I looked at her pointedly. "Get in the bath and relax."

I shut the door behind me, hoping she would heed my suggestion. Taking some time to herself just to relax and rejuvenate herself was exactly what Maddie needed. It would be good for her to just let everything go and not have to think about it for a while.

Going into my home office, I picked up the phone and called Nik while I went through the emails on my laptop.

"Nik Nygard," he answered.

"Hey, Nik. It's Toby," I said.

"Hey, Toby. Where are you having lunch? Must be good since you've been gone for almost an hour and a half."

That was exceedingly unusual for me. More often than not I just ate my lunch right at my desk. If it was a day when I wasn't, I ran to the diner and was usually back in less than half an hour.

"I'm actually calling to let you know I'm going to be out for the rest of the day. With Maddie. I need you to relay a message to the marketing department. Tell Ethan she's working on a special project with me," I told him.

Nik snickered. "I can only imagine the type of special project the two of you are working on together. Definitely not something you want to do right here in the office," he joked.

"It's not like that," I told him. "Maddie is going through some pretty serious personal issues, and I'm trying to help her work through them. She's having a hard time with it, and I hope to be able to help her figure it out."

"Oh. I'm sorry. I shouldn't have joked like that," Nik said, sounding almost embarrassed.

Nik Nygard didn't get embarrassed, so even a hint of it seemed like a big deal.

"It's all right," I told him. "You didn't know."

"Do you need any help? Anything I can do?" he asked.

"I don't think so," I told him.

"All right. Well, if you come up with something, I'm happy to help in whatever way I can," Nik said.

"Thanks. I think I have a handle on it, but I'll let you know if I need anything," I told him.

We got off the phone, and I continued to work on my computer for the next hour before heading into the kitchen to put a kettle on the stove to heat for tea. When it was boiling, I poured it into a cup and added a tea strainer with peppermint tea. It steeped on the way to my bathroom and smelled amazing by the time I got there. I knocked on the door, but Maddie didn't answer. Thinking she might have zoned out a little, I knocked again, harder this time. Still no answer. I immediately started worrying something had happened to her. No longer caring about propriety, I opened the door and stepped inside.

My shoulders relaxed and I let out a sigh of relief when I saw Maddie in the tub, her eyes closed but her chest rising and falling peacefully. The bubbles had dissipated, and most of the creamy foam had disappeared, revealing her flushed, naked skin. She slept soundly right there in the water; her head rested on a rolled-up towel against the side. My eyes devoured her body, and I ached to touch her, but I didn't want to intrude. I walked up to the tub and carefully set the teacup on the edge. Retreating as quietly as I could, I closed the door behind me and went back to my office. I tried to concentrate on work, but my erection distracted me, keeping my thoughts drifting back to Maddie in that tub.

Finally, I couldn't resist seeing her any longer. I went back to the bedroom and perched on the edge of the bed, debating when to wake Maddie.

I didn't wake up softly and gradually. There was no fluttering of my eyelashes and easing out of sleep. I snapped awake in an instant and realized with embarrassment I had fallen asleep in Toby's tub. He'd told me to get in and relax, and apparently, I'd taken those instructions very seriously, but it made sense. I had been sleeping so little lately, it was to be expected I would pass out as soon as my mind and body finally relaxed. The hot water and soothing bubbles and oils did their job better than expected. A warm new scent touched my nose, and I looked down toward the end of the tub. A teacup sat on the edge near my feet. Steam still trailed up out of it, telling me the tea inside was still hot and the cup had only been placed there recently.

Where did it come from? Did Toby come into the bathroom while I was bathing? Did he see me sleeping and just stand there gawking? Suddenly angry, I stood up out of the water and climbed from the tub. I grabbed one of the soft towels he'd set aside for me and dried my skin. Ignoring the robe he hung from the back of the door, I got back into the clothes I'd taken off and folded onto the counter. When I was dressed again, I stormed out of the bathroom and found Toby sitting on the edge of the bed. He looked at me with a soft smile, but I stepped up to him fiercely.

"I don't appreciate you coming into the bathroom and leering at me while I'm asleep in the tub," I said. "Is that why you encouraged me to get in? You wanted to be able to come in and get a look?"

Toby at least had the decency to look ashamed.

"I've been working for over an hour and hadn't heard anything from you. I thought you might like some peppermint tea to relax more, so I made you some. But I knocked several times and you didn't answer. I was worried about you, so I went in. I'm sorry. But I didn't just stand there. I set the tea down and left," he told me.

"You left to lurk in your room and wait for me to come out? Maybe hoping to catch another glance of me naked?" I asked.

I felt like I was spiraling, getting angrier and more on edge by the minute. Toby frowned, narrowing his eyes slightly as he stared back at me.

"Maddie, you're being silly. I left the bathroom within a couple of seconds of me going in, then I came back out here. I haven't been sitting here for some huge length of time lying in wait. I was trying to decide whether to wake you up or let you keep sleeping. You seemed so peaceful and comfortable, but the water had to be getting cold," he said.

I rolled my eyes. I put enough enthusiasm into the gesture to get a glimpse into the open closet. It definitely wasn't what I was expecting. Toby's suits and shirts were there. Even a selection of sweaters and what looked like a few casual shirts. Those I knew I'd see there. But it was the dresses lined up on the closet bar next to his clothes that caught my attention and made my stomach twist.

Why were there dresses in Toby's closet?

I took a couple of steps toward the open door and pointed at the clothes.

"What's that?" I asked. "Why do you have dresses in there?"

"I hired a personal shopper make some purchases for me when you agreed to our fake marriage," he explained as if it was the most normal and understandable thing in the world. My eyes widened and I strode across the room to the closet. Grabbing one of the dresses, I checked the label. Then I checked the dress beside it, then the suit beside that, and finally a gorgeous cream-colored sweater. All the clothes were in my size. And all were designer. These items were far more expensive than my own clothes. Far more expensive than anything I would have ever been able to afford.

What the fuck was going on?

That's when I really started to notice the details of my surroundings. At first, Toby's apartment just looked massive and expensive, filled with expertly put-together decor. The longer I looked at it, though, the more a few things stood out to me. Here and there throughout the room some details were out of place with the rest of the house's vibe. Little feminine touches that weren't like Toby and I knew he wouldn't choose for himself.

Realization started to settle in, and I turned to look at him. I knew my expression said I thought he was out of his mind. Truth was, I *did* think he'd lost his mind. This was unbelievable.

"You're almost worse than Craig," I told him.

"What do you mean?" Toby asked, his eyes darkening.

"What is all this? You must be some kind of weird stalker type. How long have you actually had these things? Have you been planning this for months, waiting for your opportunity to drag me into this twisted game?" I asked.

Now it was his turn to look at me like I'd lost my mind.

"You're being ridiculous," he said. "I literally just bought this stuff. We agreed to pretend we were married, and you were talking about the details and things people would look for to believe a couple is together. I figured one of those things was looking like they actually share the same space. I figured it would be good to have the appearance that we lived together, even if you maintained your apartment, in case your ex became suspicious."

I huffed an exasperated breath, no longer sure who I could trust. Taking a few steps back away from him, I waved my hands in the air in front of me and held them out to my sides like I was declaring myself innocent of the situation unfolding in front of me.

"The fake marriage is off," I announced. "I'll handle everything on my own from here."

Toby came close, towering over me.

"You're overreacting," he said to me in a controlled, even tone. "I'm not a stalker. I'm your friend. I've been the one trying to help you." His voice dropped lower, and he spoke to me softly. "It's a shame Craig did such a number on you that you can't even trust the people who care about you. Like me."

He reached out and cupped his hands around my face. I didn't move away or try to stop him, but I held in a big breath to try to get my emotions under control. As I let it out, my anger slipped away, replaced by tight, sizzling sexual tension. I knew in my heart Toby wasn't like Craig. He wouldn't do anything to hurt me, not in any way. She was just trying to help, and I was acting like a raving lunatic, when I should be grateful that I had someone on my side.

"I'm sorry, Toby," I said. I stepped up closer to him again and rested my head on his chest. "I'm just not used to being close to or able to trust anyone. I haven't dated anyone since Craig. I've focused only on my career because it's easier than dealing with emotions. I was always afraid I would find another man just like him and be in the same, if not a worse situation than I was. It's not easy for me to open up."

Toby gave me a soft smile and kissed my forehead.

"I am a safe person for you, Maddie. I will always be here if you need me. No matter what you're going through, if there's ever anything I can do for you or any way I can make things easier for you, I'm here." I stared at him, my eyes dropping to his lips and tracing them.

"Thank you," I told him.

I continued to stare at his mouth, and I saw it turn up slightly.

"If you keep looking at me like that, I won't be held responsible for what happens next," he warned.

I smiled, then pulled up onto the balls of my feet to press my lips to his. With a groan, he took control of the kiss, deepening it. Our lips touched again, and his velvety voice groaned once more as his hand slipped behind me, cupping my ass and bringing me closer to him. My arms wrapped around his neck, but now they seemed to move on their own, pulling at his collar to loosen his shirt as I tried to yank it over his head. Toby let go of me and raised his arms so I could pull it off, and my fingers ran down his chest, feeling every ripple of muscle and snaking their way to his belt.

With a pull, it loosened, and I unraveled it easily, grasping at the button of his pants. I didn't even realize we were moving until Toby pushed me against the wall, our lips finding each other again.

Our tongues twisted into each other, hungrily searching as our hands roamed each other's bodies. His found the belt tied at the waist of my wrap dress and yanked, opening it up so it fell to my sides. I relaxed my shoulders to let it fall off me, and Toby leaned back to take me in as I peeled away my bra and panties. I relished the passion in his eyes as he traced the curve of my breasts with his eyes and then ran his hands up my stomach to meet them. He crushed back into me again with a kiss, and I could feel the thick erection in his pants, begging to be freed. I worked at the button of the pants but was having trouble with it, when his hand came down to join mine. I lifted up on my toes as Toby worked his button and zipper open and they fell to the floor. His throbbing cock released out into the air, and I clasped my hands over it greedily. I stroked him as he pushed closer into me, the tip of his head brushing against my core.

Suddenly, his hands were underneath me, lifting me and pushing me against the wall with his weight. My legs wrapped around him automatically, not because of fear he would drop me, but in anticipation of what this position meant. Without wasting a moment, he thrust upward and filled me deeply and my eyes rolled back. My arms clenched around his neck, and my thighs squeezed his hips as he pressed his mouth against mine and thrust again. His fingers kneaded my ass with every push, and small whim-pering sounds soon filled the room.

I was enveloped by him, smothered in the best way imaginable, as he held on to me tightly for the next thrust. I reached back and held the wall, pushing my chest up and into his watering, waiting mouth. His tongue swirled around one nipple before he took it into his mouth, tongue flicking as he continued to push deeper into me. With a sudden spin, he turned away from the wall and carried me to the bed, where he sat me gently down on the edge and stepped back, finally kicking the pants off his legs.

CHAPTER 15

TOBY

I could barely contain my excitement, and when I sat Maddie down on the edge of the bed to finally remove my pants, I only worried she would shut it all down right then. Instead, I saw her eyes widen and a smile slide across her lips as I got naked in front of her. I took a step closer, wanting to lay her down and rediscover the intoxicating feeling of being inside of her. Before I could, her hand reached out and wrapped around my engorged cock. Placing one hand on my shoulder, gently, she led me to sit down on the bed beside her, and she turned, sitting on her knees below me.

Her lips brushed my thigh, then moved to the other, her tongue sliding out to create a trail on either side. Gradually, she moved up, closer to my cock, which she stroked slowly and deliberately. As much as I wanted to take her body immediately, to wrap myself in it and cocoon myself, she was decidedly taking her time. I tried to close my eyes to focus on the sensation, but they popped back open again a moment later. I didn't want to close my eyes and miss a single second of watching her. Her tongue swirled at the base of my cock, and she ran her lips up and down it, blowing soft hot air until she made her way to the head. Twirling her tongue around it, she took it in her mouth and the warmth, and the wetness of her worship nearly made me explode right then.

I groaned and a little giggle came from her throat, the vibration working its way down my shaft and sending me even closer to an orgasm. Plunging down, she took me deeply, the head of my cock brushing the back of her throat and her tongue slipping out below to slide across the base. I reached for her, placing a hand in her hair as she began to stroke me with her lips, guiding her in a slow and incredibly intense rhythm. Her eyes closed as she began to work me with her hand as well, and I felt like I might not hold on for much longer. Moments of bliss bled away until I couldn't take it any longer, and I pulled her by her arms back up to me.

She straddled me my stomach, and I grasped her by her ass, gently easing her down until she was sliding her burning hot core across my shaft. With a little lift, she positioned herself above me and sank down onto me, letting me fill her again. This time my groan was met by one of her own, as she rocked, riding me. One hand pressed down on my chest, while the other reached back to hold on to my thigh. I licked the pad of my thumb and slid through the folds of her center until I found her swollen clit. Maddie gasped as I swirled around it, and her hips moved faster, taking me deeper and harder into her. I tensed my hips to push up and could feel her walls stretching to accommodate me.

Her moan was the sexiest sound I had ever heard, and I felt like I couldn't wait any longer. My excitement and giddiness at finally touching her again, feeling her lips against mine, smelling her skin, it was more than I could bear already. But the sound of her pleasure, unchained and uninhibited, her body rocking on top of mine, pushed me beyond the threshold of control. I sat up, pulling her close to me, and spun her around, laying her down on the bed and eliciting another giggle from deep within her. The playfulness combined with the sultriness of her body edged me even closer to a frenzy.

I pulled Maddie's legs up so that her ankles rested on my shoulders, and I thrust deep within her. She cried out and her fingernails sank into my shoulder blades. I repeated the motion, pushing into her as deeply as I could go, and our hips ground into one another. Our eyes locked as I thrust again, beginning to move in a rhythm dictated by the need and desire both of us had for each other. Her mouth opened slightly, as if to moan again, but no sound came out, and her legs began to tremble. I knew she was coming close to another orgasm, and the knowledge of that fact drove me even wilder.

The thrusts grew faster, wilder, and a low grumble came from deep within me as I relished in the sight of her. She was writhing, curling underneath me as she began to tumble into a deep and satisfying climax, and I increased my speed to match her. I wanted to climax with her, and feel her pulse around me as I exploded inside of her. Her hands reached up to wrap around my neck, and I pulled her into me by the small of her back, slamming into her with a fury of desire.

Her hair fell over her face, still wet from the bathtub, and her eyes peered out at me from between the strands. Her body heaved and her core was slick and hot and welcoming. She was ready but waiting for me, and she knew I was close. I wouldn't keep her long. With a roar, I plunged deeply into her, my body convulsing as I emptied myself inside her, her body milking me as she climaxed along with me. Her voice rose to a fevered pitch, and one hand grasped at the sheets of the bed, pulling them up in her tight fist as our bodies vibrated and hummed in tune with the other.

When I was finally spent, empty and delirious from delight, I settled into her. She wrapped her arms around me, and I listened to her heart as it slowed down from its furious beat to a slow, contented one.

CHAPTER 16

We lay there for several long, silent moments, breathing heavily and staring up at the ceiling. It seemed like each of us was lost in our own thoughts, and I started to worry her thoughts were going down the dark rabbit hole again. I was concerned at any second she was going to change her mind again and scurry off the way she did the last time. But when I turned to her, she was smiling. I smiled back at her, feeling my heart swelling in my chest. This was so much more than just my incredible attraction to her or the chemistry we had. I lusted after, but in that moment, I also realized just how deeply I cared about her as well.

Wanting to take care of her and protect her wasn't just worrying about a woman in an uncomfortable situation with her ex. My need to defend her and ensure she was safe came from my feelings for her, and I wanted nothing more than to keep those feelings going. The fact that she was still lying in bed beside me and hadn't jumped up and disappeared was a good start. The smile on her face made it even better. I reached out and ran my hand down the side of her face, brushing the pad of my thumb across her soft lips. Her eyes drifted closed, and she kissed my fingertips. It was a comforting, content moment, and I felt like I could gather Maddie up in my arms and spend the rest of the day just tangled there together.

Then, a loud grumbling from her stomach put an end to that thought. We laughed and she shook her head, like she was silently chastising her stomach for being so rude and ruining the whole mood of our moment together.

"I guess I'm hungry," she said.

I nodded. "I would think so. You didn't have any lunch. As a matter of fact, if I remember correctly, you laid the smackdown on Craig and made your Oscar-worthy exit before we even got our food," I said.

Maddie gave a mock gasp of offense, then laughed again.

"It was a pretty good exit. I'll give myself that, but it was justified," she said.

"It was definitely justified. There's no question about that. But now, I should probably feed you. Can't have you withering away or not having any strength or energy," I said, sitting up and swinging my legs over the side of the bed.

"Strength and energy?" she asked. "Are we going hiking later?"

I glanced back over my shoulder at her and saw the mischievous smile on her face. I winked and got up to go into the bathroom. Grabbing the robe off the hook on the back of the door, I brought it back into the bedroom and tossed it onto Maddie. She giggled and got up to put it on. I took my own robe from the closet and tied it around my waist before reaching for her. I had only been out of the bed for a matter of seconds, but it already felt like too long to not be touching her. I pulled her into a hug and kissed her. She sighed and relaxed into my embrace as I rested my head on hers.

"Come on," I said into the top of her head. "Let's go find something to eat."

We headed into the kitchen, and I started searching through the cabinets.

"What, no cook?" Maddie teased.

"Didn't come with the apartment," I told her, choosing a different cabinet to pillage. "But it's still on my list." I leaned around the cabinet door to look at her. "Where do you shop for one of those?"

She shook her head. "I don't think you can shop for them."

I shrugged and leaned back into the cabinet. "Then I guess I'll just have to do without."

An idea for dinner popped into my head, and I started gathering ingredients from the cabinets. Piling them up on the counter, I went to the refrigerator and pulled out a few more things. When I had everything I needed, I took out a cutting board and knife. Maddie watched me with a look of surprise on her face as I picked up an onion and quickly diced it. I pushed the pieces aside and reached for another one. When I was finished with the onions and reached for a carrot, I glanced at her again. She was still staring at me.

"What?" I asked. "Never seen somebody chopping up vegetables before?"

"Not an important businessman like you, no. I wouldn't think someone like you would be standing around in their own kitchen chopping vegetables. It just doesn't seem like your type of skill set," she told me.

I laughed and slid the carrots to the side before going for a potato. "Well, I wasn't always an important businessman.

And I learned to cook when I was young. It's something my grandmother taught me. Being kind of the nerdy type, I didn't really spend a lot of time outside. So I would go into the kitchen with her and watch her. As I got older, she started letting me help her do things, and eventually I was cooking whole meals with her. I kept it up on through my teens. It's something I really enjoy. It relaxes me and lets me think about other things."

"I'm impressed," Maddie said. She watched me for a few more seconds. "Can I help?"

"Sure," I said. "Why don't you go into that cabinet and get out a big pot for water. Then get out a stainless-steel pan so we can brown the meat."

She followed my instructions, and we went to work cooking dinner together. It felt comfortable and natural like we'd done it a thousand times before. The domestic scene made me smile, and I knew I wanted many more evenings just like this. I liked having her in my space. She made even the smallest activities of daily life seem more important and enjoyable.

I tended to be the type of person who ate a lot of my meals leaned up against the kitchen counter or curled up on the living room sofa watching trashy TV I'd probably lie about later. Not Toby. When we finished cooking the beef stew, he put everything in serving dishes and brought it over to the heavy wood table in the center of the formal dining room. He set each place, then pulled out my chair for me. I sat down and waited for him to settle in place before picking up my fork and sampling the food. It smelled incredible, and I'd been waiting anxiously to taste it ever since he'd started cooking. Just like I expected it to be, it was absolutely delicious. I quickly tasted everything, then looked up and saw him smiling at me.

"Do you like it?" he asked.

"It's amazing," I told him. "You know, most nights I'd be sitting in my living room probably eating either leftovers I nuked in the microwave or something I ordered, watching a reality TV show I'd turn into a documentary before I told anybody about it tomorrow."

Toby laughed.

"So, every time you've talked about watching military history shows?"

"Oh. That soapy period drama where everybody wears ball attire and sweeps around having clandestine affairs," I told him.

"Science mini-series?"

"Cooking competitions," I revealed.

"So, what you're telling me is you lie about everything you watch?" He asked the question with a hint of a smile as he swirled wine in his glass before taking a sip.

"Not lying," I clarified. "Marketing. I put a spin on it to make it more appealing to the mass audience."

"Perfect. Okay. How about National Geographic?"

"Real Housewives. Every time," I said, taking another bite.

He laughed again. "Wow. Harsh."

I shrugged. "If the Gucci fits. Have you seen those women go at it? Sometimes I'm afraid one of them is going to scalp the other one just with their acrylic nails. It gets pretty intense."

"I've never actually seen one of those shows, so I'm just going to have to take your word for it," he told me.

"All right, so that's my dirty little secret. I spend my alone time watching inane TV while eating in my sweats. How about you? What do you do around here when no one is around to see it?" I asked.

Toby tilted his head and went back to swirling his wine like he was deep in thought.

"Hmmmm..."

"Oh, come on. You know you have something. Everybody does. Spill," I said.

"Okay, okay," he said, setting down his glass and holding up his hands like he was surrendering. "I read comic books."

I stared at him over my full fork for a beat.

"Comic books?"

"Yes," he said. "I am a grown man who still collects comic books. Of course, since I've started making so much more money, my collection has gotten a little more impressive than it used to be. But there's a room in the back of the apartment that I called a second library. It sounds really impressive until you realize it only has about ten books and the rest are full of display cases of comic books."

I tried to be understanding. After all, I did just confess my own embarrassing entertainment secret, but I couldn't help it. I burst out laughing. It was so unexpected, just like him taking mastery over the kitchen like he had. All of it didn't push me off in any way. If anything, it just made me like him even more. Every time I learned something new about Toby, he just became more appealing. Soon we fell into a comfortable conversation talking about our favorite entertainment, places we'd like to vacation, and other little details about ourselves we hadn't shared the other night. After a while, the conversation lulled, and we focused on eating for a few quiet moments.

"What are your plans for what to do about your sister and Craig?" Toby suddenly asked.

It took the fun and lightness of the evening right out of me. I frowned, setting down my silverware as my appetite abandoned me.

"I can't even believe Megan is seeing him. What would possess her to do that? Especially after the hell he put me through. I'm lost, but I'm going to get to the bottom of things with the two of them. I need to figure out what the hell is going on, then I'll decide what I'm going to do about it."

Standing up sharply from the table, I returned to the bedroom and dug out my phone. Sitting on the edge of the bed, I called Megan. Out of the corner of my eye, I could see Toby walk up to the doorway and lean against it. It didn't bother me that he was listening to the conversation. We were together in so many ways, so he might as well know what was going on. The phone rang several times before Megan picked up. I could barely hear her voice over the noise from wherever she was. I rolled my eyes.

"Are you at another party?" I asked.

My sister let out a dramatic sigh.

"My classes have been so incredibly hard. It's just so much pressure and stress. Studying just about takes everything out of me. You have no idea ..." she started, but I cut her off.

"Craig came to see me today," I say. "He says the two of you are getting married."

That was enough to completely end her rambling. She didn't say anything, and I listened to her raucous surroundings for a few seconds. She didn't respond.

"Megan?" I said. Still nothing. "Megan?"

Calling her name louder into the phone didn't have any effect. There was still no response, and after another few seconds of silence from her on the other end of the line, the call disconnected. I let out an exasperated sigh. This was so fucking typical of my little sister. She didn't like what was going on or that someone was confronting her about something, so she threw a temper tantrum and ran away. But I wasn't going to let her get away with it. This was more than just her skipping classes or letting her grades slip because she wasn't paying attention. This wasn't her running her car into the mailbox after having her license suspended for three days or sneaking liquor to her friends after the prom.

It wasn't just a stupid decision or a mistake she could get over quickly. If Craig was telling the truth and she actually was planning on marrying him, she was completely throwing her life away. Not to mention that she's putting herself at serious risk.

I dialed her phone again and listened to it ring several times. Hanging up before the voicemail clicked on, I called twice more. It did the same thing. The fourth time, it went straight to voicemail. I tried one more time, wondering if it was possible if she was calling me at the same moment. When it went straight to voicemail again, I knew that wasn't the case. She had tired of me trying to get to her and turned off her phone. This time, I let voicemail pick up.

"Megan, I don't know what the hell you think you're doing, but this is ridiculous. When you talked to me the other day, you said he sent the message that he would see me soon and had an important question to ask me. You called the man Coach Shelton. It is seriously fucked-up for you to be playing games like this. You need to get your shit together, put on your big-girl panties, and face up to whatever the hell kind of mess you've gotten yourself into now. You are being absurd trying to get attention and cause drama with this. You think you can just toy with people to get the attention you want and get your way. Then when you're done, you believe it will all go away. And that there won't be any consequences. Well, let me tell you, little sister, that's not the case. It's time to grow up and face real life. Call me back immediately and explain yourself."

When I was done with the message, I hung up and flung the phone onto the bed beside me. It didn't have quite the same impact and panache as slamming down the receiver of an old-school landline phone, but it was the best I could do in this situation. Throwing my arms out to my sides, I tossed myself backward and landed on the mattress with a loud groan.

A creative stream of profanity made Toby laugh. He pushed away from the doorframe and walked over to the bed. Sitting down beside me, he reached out and patted my thigh comfortingly.

"So, I guess your sister didn't feel much like talking?" he asked.

"You can put it that way. It's convenient, considering Megan usually never stops complaining. Talking about herself and all of her delusions about how difficult her life is in college is her favorite sport," I told him.

"That message was pretty strongly worded," he said.

"Nothing she hasn't heard before," I said. "Well, it might have been a little bit stronger than my usual check-in. I think the situation warrants it."

"Do you think she's going to call you back?" he asked.

I shook my head, still staring up at the ceiling and trying to wrap my mind around everything that had happened in the last couple of days. There was no chance I was getting a phone call back from Megan anytime soon.

"No. Not in the next couple of weeks, anyway. She's not the type of person to be mature and confront her situations head-on. She does the same thing now that she did when she was a little girl. She runs away and hides when she's in trouble. Then she waits until she figures the worst has passed and the heat is off and reemerges like nothing ever happened. That's likely what's going to happen now. I could sit around and wait for her. I could call her back a bunch of times. It's not going to do any good. As long as she thinks I'm upset with her and I'm continuing to demand she explain what's going on, she's going to pretend I don't exist," I said.

"So, she's basically going to put her hands over her eyes and say she can't see you, so you can't see her?" he asked.

I let out a short laugh.

"Essentially. But, I guarantee you if I did let that happen, in two or three weeks she'd call with another life crisis that could be the plot of a *Sweet Valley High* book if the twins started drinking and wearing barely enough clothing for a Barbie," I told him.

"I'm not sure I know what that means."

I laughed again. "I'll get you a couple of books for your second library."

"All right but let me know ahead of time. I'm going to have to move out a couple books I already have in there to make sure I have space," he joked.

"Will do." I let out a sigh as my mind returned to the problem at hand. "She's never going to be up-front about this, which actually worries me more. If she was just pretending to be in a relationship with Craig to get my attention, she would want to talk about it. She wouldn't be burying her head in the sand and waiting until she thinks I forgot so she can pop back up with her special brand of ridiculous drama."

I was making fun of her, but it was only to keep myself from crying. In truth, I was incredibly worried about her and needed to end the situation as fast as possible.

"So, what are you going to do about it?" Toby asked.

I turned my head to the side to look at him.

"She's going to keep running and avoiding me, which means only one thing. I will have to go home to Kansas to deal with this in person."

Maddie let out a long, defeated breath and turned her face back up toward the ceiling. I lay down beside her, inching across the mattress so my body was close to hers and our heads just touched. It was a familiar kind of connection that struck me with its intimacy. I was surprised to be able to feel so close to her and so bonded just lying together this way. None of my other relationships had ever had this type of feeling. Not that I had a huge array of former girlfriends to compare the feeling to. But in those few instances, I'd never felt this level of comfort, contentment, and acceptance. It was wonderful, but it also meant the tugging feeling as I realized she'd be leaving soon. I wasn't going to get to hide her away from the rest of the world and keep her all to myself as I dreamed.

"So, what's your plan?" I asked after a few seconds of contemplative silence.

I rolled onto my side and rose up on my elbow so I could look down at her. Even just like that, she was so beautiful.

She gazed up into my face and shook her head. Her shoulders lifted and fell against the bed just slightly.

"I'm not sure," she admitted. "It's all coming so fast. Honestly, as much as I'm not looking forward to this, I probably shouldn't wait. The longer I delay, the more awkward it's going to get and the higher the chances of something happening."

A long breath seemed to deflate Maddie, and she moved closer so that she was pressed up against me. I didn't ask what she meant when she said there were higher chances of something happening. She didn't have to say it for me to understand what she was trying to say. I didn't want the details. Not right now. If I had to listen to her describe what she worried Craig could do to her little sister, it would force me to confront what he did to her, and that wasn't something I could handle. I didn't trust myself if I had that information. It was enough to just know she was worried about Megan and didn't want to think of her in a situation like what she'd gone through.

"What do you want to do?" I asked.

"I'm going to book a flight as soon as I can be ready, take a couple days off, and go back to Kansas to confront my sister. Another good thing about me getting it done as soon as possible is I can get there while Craig is still in New York. I really don't need him to be there when this all goes down," she said.

"You decide when you want to go, and we'll get the plans in place. I'm sure something can be arranged at work to cover for us," I told her.

Maddie propped herself up and looked at me, her expression confused.

"Us?" she asked.

I nodded matter-of-factly. "I'm coming with you."

Rather than the happy, excited reaction I thought the announcement would get from Maddie, she shook her head.

"That won't be necessary," she said. "It's not like I'm going off into the unknown. I'm going back home to deal with my sister. You don't need to disrupt your life and put everything on hold to go with me."

"You aren't just going home, Maddie. This isn't a leisure trip or some sort of fun reunion. It's going to be a difficult visit, and you know it. You need someone with you for moral support. Besides, what if you're wrong about Craig still being in New York? He's here now, but what reason does he have to stick around here now that he's told you he's planning on marrying Megan? Especially considering the way you reacted to the news, he might have already made plans to head back there. You don't want to show up there and be surprised by him while you're alone any more than I want you to. I'm going with you," I told her in no uncertain terms.

Maddie's eyes suddenly sparkled with tears, and a light flush of red crossed her cheekbones.

"Why are you so good to me?" she asked softly. "Why are you helping me with all this? It's such a mess, and you don't have to be a part of it. There's no reason you should have to put yourself through all this."

I reached out and took her into my arms, sitting up so I could cradle her close against me. I pressed a kiss into her hair and stroked her back to comfort her.

"Of course there's a reason. You deserve to be treated well. You've been fighting alone for too long. And everyone needs help sometimes. It's part of being human, but that's not the whole reason. I care about you, Maddie. I'm always going to be here to give you support when you need it. I can't always promise I'll fully understand what's going on as soon as it happens or know what I should do. But I promise I will be there to listen to you, and when you know what I can do to help you, I'll be there to do it."

I guided her away from me and looked into her eyes. Holding her face in my hands, I used my thumbs to brush away the tears sliding down along her cheeks. She nuzzled her face into my palm, and I leaned in to kiss her. I only meant it to be an encouragement, but Maddie leaned into it. She pressed her lips harder against mine, seeking more of the kiss. I complied eagerly, sliding my hands around her waist and deepening the kiss as I lowered her down onto the bed.

I hovered above her, the bottom half of my body slowly sinking down, pressing her into the comfort and refuge of the bed. Her lips parted and my tongue slid inside to explore hers yet again. No matter how many times I tasted her, it was never enough, and our kiss ripened the desire to engulf her, envelop her, and meld into one being. I wanted to take away her fears, and her worries, and replace them with the ever-deepening desire for each other.

My lips moved from her mouth to her neck, and I trailed down it to her collarbone. Sweeping my tongue across it, I lapped up the salty sweat hungrily, and my throbbing erection began to brush against. I could feel the heat from beneath her robe, and I wanted to remove it, to be completely naked against her skin and feel every cell of her skin against mine. But I wanted to control myself more. To show her how safe, how protected she was with me, I needed to take this moment slowly, tenderly. I needed to show her there was no rush, no forcefulness in my hunger for her, only longing and strength and safety.

Kissing across her chest, I swept my tongue up the little dip in the center of her neck before moving down. Her chest heaved toward me as she ground her hips into me. She wanted me inside her as much as I wanted it, but I paced myself. Pushing myself up on my knees, I untied the belt around my waist and then slipped the robe off my shoulders. Her eyes flickered from my chest to my bulge, and she lifted her hand to brush over it. I tossed the robe aside, and she began to work on her own, but I pulled her hands off. Reaching down gently, I clasped the belt in my teeth and untied it with my mouth, my hands sliding into hers and our fingers interlacing.

As I parted her robe, she opened herself up to me, presenting her most intimate parts, and I knelt down between her legs. She pulled her knees up so her feet rested on the sides of my shoulders, and I blew a stream of hot breath along her center. Her toes curled, and I took the invitation to sweep my tongue along her opening, tracing her fully before arriving back at the delicate folds above.

Maddie's hands slipped into my hair, and she pulled me into her, my tongue sliding directly to the pearl in the center. One hand slid below, and I slipped two fingers inside her as I licked her in a soft but firm rhythm. Her body arched, and her legs shook as she cascaded into an orgasm, a whimper escaping her mouth before her thighs clenched around my head.

Maddie's eyes shut as her body pulsed, and she pulled me up. More than anything right then, I needed to be inside of her, and she grasped at my hips to get to me faster. I sat up on my knees in front of her. My rock-hard erection springing forth. She clasped it at the base and milked it for a moment. Eliciting a moan of pleasure, and the sound seemed to make her even more desperate for the closeness. Reaching up with her other hand, she tried to pull me down to her, but I resisted, and for a moment I just sat there, eyes

following every curve of her body, exalting her with attention. Without breaking eye contact with her, I slipped
myself under the covers and held them open for Maddie.
She wiggled between the sheets, and we embraced in the
center of the bed, our pace now slowed but the passion of
the moment only increasing.

Our lips played across each other, meeting again and
again as if to remind each other of the intensity of our kiss. I
slid over again, pressing my weight into her, but this time
my body and hers had nothing between them. Her skin was
warm and comforting against mine, and I brushed across
her body to put myself between her thighs. Her nipples
hardened at the contact with my skin. My cock pressed
against her core as my elbows propped me up, and the slick
warmth there beckoned me to plunge deep inside. Yet, I did
not rush as I slid my thick, engorged cock along her folds,
allowing her body to cover it with the slick fluids of her
pussy. Maddie's body tingled in anticipation, and heat rose
up her chest to burn my cheeks. They were flush, and her
eyes were wide, waiting, beckoning me. She took a deep
breath in while I positioned myself, and it escaped fiercely
from her lips as I plunged inside.

I held himself there for a moment, allowing her walls to
open further for me, to cradle me inside of her. Our eyes
were still locked onto one another as I leaned in to place my
lips on hers. As our kiss deepened, I pulled back and
plunged again, beginning a rhythm that lit her body up
making her writhe and hold her breath as she adjusted for
my girth. She wrapped her legs around my waist, and I
leaned into it, driving even deeper inside her, and she
clenched her thighs to hold me there for a moment before
relaxing and letting me continue to stroke into her.

CHAPTER 19

MADDIE

My eyes closed as I let myself disappear into the intense pleasure he was enthralling me in. Toby was taking his time, letting me relax into the moment rather than attack with frenzied passion. It was a comforting pace, allowing me to enjoy every second, every bit of weight of his body on mine, every stretch of my walls to accommodate him. He buried his face in my chest and took a nipple into his mouth, lavishing it with attention while his hands made their way down to cup my ass. He held me up by the hips, inches above the bed, while my head rested on the pillows and I ran my nails lightly up his back. His moan of pleasure made me thrust my hips up to meet him, and I could feel him stretching me even further.

Toby's hands slid to my hips, and he pulled his knees under me so that I rested on them while he rolled his hips. His strong, sure grip pulled me gently but firmly into each thrust, and I arched back in a dizzying wave of ecstasy. The rhythm increased and a low grunt of effort tumbled from his lips, as I clenched my legs around him and pulled myself up so that I was sitting on him. Instead of rolling to his back, he pulled one arm around me and cupped me with the other, lifting me, controlling the pace and keeping it steady. Sweat began to make our bodies slick, and my eyes zeroed in on a bead running down the side of his neck. I flicked out my tongue to catch it, and the sensation of my hot breath on his skin must have awoken a deeper hunger within him. He increased the speed, and soon I felt another powerful surge coursing through me.

Suddenly, he lifted one of my legs and turned me, never leaving his place inside me, so that my back was to him. His arms wrapped around me, one pulling me at my hips and the other sliding up to cup my breast. We slid back down to the bed and lay there, my body arching back and aching for him to continue. His thrusts were not desperate or uncontrolled, but deep and filling, and I let out a cry as he increased the speed. His tongue played on my sensitive nipple before he let go, bringing his lips to the back of my neck and sliding his tongue to the lobe of my ear. The rocking of his hips grew faster, and his hands clenched my hips, pulling me into him with each movement. I felt myself losing control again and knew I was about to topple over the edge of another orgasm when I felt his cock pulse inside me. He drove himself deep within me, and his grip tightened, holding me in place as he spilled into me, locked in place. I thrust my hand out to push against the wall, grinding myself even deeper onto him and riding the wave of the orgasm until my body stopped shaking and I melted back into him, our hearts beating heavily, but slowing as we relaxed into the sweat-soaked sheets and listened to each other breathe.

I wanted to just stay right there and not move for as long as possible. It was the type of perfect moment that made everything seem to disappear. There was nothing to worry about when I was in his arms. I didn't have to think about anything else that was going on, or even think about what might happen next. If I could just keep savoring the feeling of his skin and the sound of his heart, everything was fine.

All too soon, that had to come to an end. Toby nuzzled closer and kissed me on the side of my head before pulling away from me.

"I'm going to go ahead and send some emails to the office to let them know that we'll be out for a few days. You're right about it being good for us to get going as soon as possible. Look for flights and see if there are any available tomorrow morning. If not, I'll arrange a private flight for us. I'll let the office know we'll be out for at least a week while we manage a personal issue. This way they won't ask any questions or try to get too involved," he said.

I felt a frisson of anxiety pick up the hair on my skin and make my stomach turn slightly. The peace and comfort I was feeling just a few seconds before disappeared, and I was left wondering what people were going to think. As soon as they got an email from Toby saying we were dealing with a personal matter, tongues were going to start wagging, and the water cooler talk was going to reach epic levels. Especially coming on the heels of the mind-boggling revelation of Nik and Jane's relationship, it was going to seem instantly scandalous. Everyone was clamoring for another juicy bit of office gossip, and I didn't want anyone thinking that way about me.

Toby started to stand up, and I reached for his arm to stop him.

"Can you think of a different way to word it?" I asked.

"Why?" he asked.

"I don't want people at the office to know you're helping me with a personal matter. Now that you know my background and what I came from, you understand even better how important my career is to me. I worked hard to get my position, and I don't want people to think I'm getting special favors from the boss," I told him.

Toby looked disappointed. I knew he didn't have a problem with anyone at the office attaching us to each other, and he couldn't see the risk of people talking. He was too kind to think that way. Since he wasn't the type of person to think badly on others or to think a person would leverage a relationship for personal gain in the office, he wouldn't automatically think that of others. Finally, he gave a slight nod.

"Alright," he agreed. "I promise I'll be discreet."

He got out of bed and slipped back into his robe. I stayed there in bed, trying to hold on to as much of the warmth from his side as I could. I wasn't sure what to do. The logical, responsible part of my brain knew I should get dressed and go home to pack so I could be ready to leave for Kansas as soon as possible, but I really didn't want to be alone at home that night. The thought of leaving Toby and going into my empty apartment left me feeling cold. I combated the feeling by snuggling down under the blankets and pretending nothing else existed.

A few minutes later, Toby came back into the room, and I heard his robe hit the floor. Happiness warmed me as he climbed back into the bed with me and curled me up into his arms. I felt safe when he held me, and I dropped almost instantly to sleep.

My sleep was surprisingly deep, and I was even more surprised to wake up in Toby's arms and realize it was morning. Snuggling closer, I enjoyed the feeling of him holding me and the familiarity of sharing the space with him. It felt so good to have him right there, to be with him in the first minutes of the day. He made a happy groaning sound as he turned and kissed the side of my neck.

"You fell asleep so fast last night you didn't get a chance to make any travel arrangements for us," he said. "But don't worry, I called my travel agent and got us a noon flight. Nonstop right to Kansas."

I giggled as he kissed the curve of my neck again.

"That doesn't leave us much time."

Toby's groan turned frustrated and dramatic as I wriggled away from him and hopped up out of bed.

"I'll call the agent and change our flight," he told me. "Just come back to bed."

I laughed and rushed around looking for my clothes. "Not happening, buddy." He made a face, and I bounced across the bed to give him a quick kiss. "I'm going to run home and pack. I'll meet you at the airport at ten-thirty."

He tried to pull me back into bed with him, but I laughed again and pulled away from him, shaking my head. Toby groaned and buried his head in the pillow for a second before looking up at me again.

"Alright. I'll send you the flight information and see you in a few hours."

I still couldn't get the smile off my face when I got to the front door of the building and headed for my apartment. My key had just slipped into my lock when movement out of the corner of my eye made me stop. I gasped as Craig came out of the shadows toward me.

"Where the fuck have you been all night?" he demanded.

I pulled my key out of the door and moved away from him, trying not to let him see me jump.

"Not that it's any of your business, but I spent the night at home with my husband," I told him.

Craig scoffed, his hands planted on his hips as he looked at me with a mocking expression in his eyes.

"That overgrown nerd isn't fit to sign your paychecks, let alone marry you," he said.

"Go away, Craig. I'm not in the mood for a chat."

I didn't want him to notice my fear or get that rush of power he always got when he tried to push me around. My resistance didn't do any good. In one sudden movement, Craig closed the space between us and grabbed me. The air burst out of me as he slammed me against the hallway wall. His hot breath seethed across my skin, and I felt a fine mist of saliva settle on me as he got within inches of my face. I wanted to close my eyes and not have to see the wildness in his stare. Blood vessels spread in violent red cracks across the whites of his eyes, and his teeth gritted so hard the muscles in his jaw twitched. My heart pounded in my chest, and I struggled to keep my breath even.

"Well, I'm not in the mood for your mouth," he said.

"What do you want?" I asked angrily.

"What I've always wanted, Maddie," he said. "You."

I shoved him hard and scrambled away from Craig as fast as I could. I managed to get out of his grip and moved toward my door. Reaching for my phone, I pulled it out so he could see it in my hand.

"Leave or I'm going to call the police," I said as force-fully as I could.

No matter how much strength I pushed into my voice, it did nothing to dissuade Craig. He laughed and took a swaggering step toward me.

"It's a good thing you aren't calling your nerd husband because you know I would demolish him," he said.

That was enough. I dialed 9-1-1 and it started ringing. Craig watched me like he was daring me to actually say something, like he didn't believe I would do anything against him.

"9-1-1, do you need fire, EMS, or police?" the operator asked.

"My ex-boyfriend is at my apartment and won't let me go inside. He grabbed me and pushed me against the wall. I fear for my safety," I said, the words coming out in a long stream.

Craig shook his head and scoffed, walking past me and disappearing down the hallway as if nothing happened. I stood there alone, gripping my phone hard enough it pushed painfully into my hand. I was trembling, and it took several seconds for the sound of the operator's voice to register again.

"Ma'am? Ma'am? Are you all right?" he asked, his voice getting louder as he went.

"I'm sorry. I'm fine. He left," I said.

I hung up, hoping they wouldn't send someone anyway. The last thing I needed right then was to have police show up at my apartment building and start questioning me. There wasn't time for that. After the confrontation, I knew even more that I needed to get to Kansas and find out what was happening with my sister.

Stuffing the phone in my pocket, I let myself into my apartment and hurried to get packed. My heart was pounding painfully in my chest and my hands were shaking, making it difficult to fold my clothes and put them in my suitcase. My mind was spinning, but I couldn't stop. Toby was waiting for me. I had to put the encounter with Craig behind me and keep going.

CHAPTER 20

TOBY

I knew I shouldn't have let Maddie go back to her apartment by herself. I should have insisted on getting myself packed and going with her. At least then we could have traveled to the airport together, and I wouldn't be standing by the check-in desks waiting for her. We agreed to meet at ten-thirty and that would give us just enough time to get through security and settle in before our noon flight. It was cutting it close as it was, but this was getting really ridiculous. Our appointed meeting time had come and gone, and there was still no sign of Maddie.

I called for the fourth time, but it rang until it went to voicemail. Several texts had already gone unanswered. It was already almost eleven. Whenever she showed up, we still needed to check our luggage, go through security, and get onto the plane. It was going to be tight as it was, and now it was getting close to being futile. I had no interest in being the person running through the airport desperately trying to catch my flight.

Of course, there was another possibility. She might not

just be running late. Craig had already shown up at her place once before. Who's to say, he wasn't waiting for her when she went back and now had her against her will somewhere. I could feel my adrenaline increase and my pulse pick up at the idea of him with her.

The thoughts rushing through my head almost convinced me to cancel our tickets, catch a cab, and go to her apartment to find out what was happening. Just as I was starting to walk away from where I'd been standing for more than half an hour, I saw Maddie coming toward me. I exhaled in relief and tried to calm myself as she approached, but something in her face still had me worried.

I wasn't anticipating her being thrilled about the trip, but her expression was even more than just not looking forward to what was ahead. She looked upset and frazzled, and immediately my hackles were up.

"What happened?" I asked.

Maddie's face didn't relax, and she shook her head, continuing past me without even pausing.

"We should really hurry up. We need to check in and get through security," she announced.

I was tempted to point out she was almost half an hour late, and that was the reason we were really coming in under the wire, but I held my tongue. Maddie was obviously upset, and I didn't want to push her. We made our way to security and found a long line winding through the area. She rolled her eyes and let her head fall forward, but I rubbed her back encouragingly. It took even longer than I expected for us to finally get all the way through the various stages of security checks, and we rushed to the gate just as the flight was boarding.

I handed the gate attendant our boarding passes, and he checked them over, nodding before handing them back and gesturing for us to go into the plane. I showed them to the next attendant waiting just beyond the door, and she led us to our seats. Maddie looked shocked to realize we were in first class.

She looked to the luxurious leather seats, then back at me.

"Seriously?" she asked.

I nodded and lifted my carry-on into the overhead compartment before picking up hers and doing the same.

"Absolutely," I said. "You would expect anything less from me?"

I winked at her playfully and gestured for her to slide in and take the window seat. When I settled into the aisle seat, I looked up at the flight attendant waiting at the ready and ordered glasses of champagne.

"I've never been in first class before," Maddie admitted. "I didn't think I would ever be able to."

The attendant arrived with the drinks, and I handed one to Maddie, who took it with an expression that said she was both impressed and relieved. That look confirmed something had happened that morning, but she wasn't talking about it.

"You deserve a bit of pampering," I told her. "This hasn't been easy for you, and I don't think it's going to get a lot better in the near future. I can't take away what you have to go through, but I might be able to make you more comfortable in the meantime."

"Thank you," she said gratefully.

I lifted my glass toward her. "A toast. To our newest adventure."

Finally, Maddie cracked a smile. The plane started taxiing, and we sat back for takeoff. Soon we were rising up through the air, and I looked over at her. She stared out the window and watched the clouds go by and New York disappear beneath us.

"I never get over the feeling of amazement when I fly," she told me.

She looked over at me and let out a sigh, her smile still there and her eyes more peaceful.

"Are you ready to tell me what happened this morning?" I asked.

Her smile instantly faded, but she didn't turn away or try to ignore the question.

"Craig was waiting for me at my apartment building when I got there," she admitted.

"He was waiting for you?" I repeated, my body tensing.

It was yet another reason I shouldn't have let her be alone. I knew Craig couldn't be trusted for even a sliver of time. If I was there with her, she wouldn't be this upset.

"Yes," she said. "I was unlocking my door, and he just kind of came out of nowhere at me. It really shook me up."

"What happened? What did he say?"

"He didn't really say much," Maddie said. "But I'm worried the situation is more complicated than I thought."

She didn't say anything else or elaborate any further. It was obvious she was done with the conversation and just wanted to relax for a little while. I ordered her another glass of champagne and let the topic go for now. She would open up to me on her own time. And when she was ready, I'd make sure I was there to listen to her and help her decide what to do next.

When Maddie talked about it, Kansas seemed like a world away from New York. Instead, the flight was surprisingly short. We were quiet the entire way. She was lost somewhere in her own thoughts, and I didn't intrude on them. I held her hand as I thought about all the ways I would destroy Craig if he hurt Maddie ever again. When we landed, I helped her get her carry-on and guided her off the plane. The airport was like a study in comparisons against the one in New York. It was so much smaller and quieter. We got our luggage from the carousel, and she started toward the rental car counters.

"I never thought I'd see the day when I had to get a rental car just to get home," she said.

"Well, you still haven't," I told her, gesturing with my head toward the man holding a sign with my name on it.

"Who's he?" she asked as we walked up to the man.

He smiled. "Good afternoon. I'm Vincent. I'll be your chauffeur. If you'll follow me, the car is waiting."

"You have a driver waiting for us?" Maddie asked. "Are you serious?"

"Like I said, you deserve a little pampering," I told her.

We got outside, and she stopped in her tracks when she saw the driver putting our luggage into the trunk of a limo.

"Go on," I told her. "Get in."

She looked at me incredulously.

"You are seriously pulling out all the stops. Don't you realize we're in a small Kansas town, not Manhattan?" she asked.

I shrugged. "My wife deserves nothing, but the best."

She smiled, a very light touch of color coming to her cheeks, then rolled her eyes. Vincent opened the back door, and Maddie slid inside. I followed her and she settled against me, her head resting on my shoulder as she enjoyed the ride. The limo brought us to the nicest hotel I could find in the area, and the driver jumped out to help us. He met a single bellhop outside the hotel and recruited him to help. Maddie looked uncomfortable watching them, so I helped her out, hoping our decoy relationship would distract her. I took her hand, and we walked into the lobby and up to the check-in desk.

"Toby Michaels," I said when the clerk greeted me.

He typed something into his computer and then nodded.

"Yes, of course. Mr. and Mrs. Michaels, we are delighted to have you. Please let me know if there is anything you need. Absolutely anything," the clerk said.

"Thank you," I replied.

When we were fully checked in, Maddie and I crossed the lobby to the elevators. She was quiet the entire time we rode. We reached the floor with the suite I reserved, and I unlocked it. When she stepped inside, she couldn't help but draw in a breath. She looked around the suite, amazed.

"Is there something wrong?"

"Wrong? Something wrong? Of course not. This place is incredible. I'm just amazed. I'm not used to the high life."

I shrugged. "Mrs. Michaels is a well-kept woman."

"And, again, you really pulled out all the stops," she said.

"We want people around here to believe we are really married. If we make a big splash about everything, everyone will just automatically come to their own conclusions," I told her.

It seemed to reassure her, but in my mind, I knew that wasn't the whole truth. Maddie deserved this. Even more than that, I wanted her to realize what it would be like to be the *real* Mrs. Michaels.

We continued to roam through the suite, and she finally found the bedroom.

"Look how comfortable the big bed looks," she said.

A mischievous smile crossed my lips, and I let go of her hand to scoop her up.

"Let's test out that theory," I suggested.

Maddie let out a squeal when she bounced across the mattress as I tossed her onto the bed. She laughed and rearranged herself so she was sitting back against the pillows. She crooked her finger at me, and I instantly grew hot. I dove into bed and gathered her in a fast, immediate kiss. Our mouths played against each other for a few seconds before I got back off and stood at the foot of the bed, gazing at her.

Maddie lay back on the bed, spreading herself out to take up as much space as possible. I looked down on her playful, beckoning smile and unbuttoned my shirt. Maddie let out an over-the-top labored sigh and closed her eyes as if she were falling asleep on the massive bed. One eye peeked open with the sound of the zipper and didn't shut again until I was naked and climbing on top of her. Wrapping her arms around my neck, she laughed softly as I brought my lips to her neck.

Her hand slid down my back as I rolled my hips into her, my hands slipping under her shirt. Flipping her shirt up, I revealed her breasts and ran my tongue across the line of her bra, tracing it. Maddie's hands slipped behind her in an attempt to unclasp it, but I stopped her. Our eyes met, and I grinned as I ran my hand behind her and undid the clasp myself in one easy motion. I leaned in and we kissed deeply, passionately, and she pushed me on one shoulder until I rolled on my back.

Lying down beside me, Maddie began trailing a line of kisses down my chest. As she did, I quickly unbuttoned her pants and she gracefully helped me slide them off her while she made her way down my abdomen. Her panties slipped off easily with her jeans, and she presented herself to me as she began to swirl her tongue along the base of my now throbbing cock. I groaned heavily, and her hand grasped my base and began to stroke me gently.

I wasn't about to let her have all the fun. I grabbed one of her legs and pulled it toward me, getting her to straddle my head. Maddie arched down toward me, bringing her sweet pussy inches from my face, and I took the opportunity to run my tongue along the crook of her leg, dragging it all the way across to the other. Next, I traced the outline of her core, noting how wet and ready for me she already was, and wanting to drive her further out of control while I had her in this position.

Maddie seemed to be thinking the same thing as she suddenly took me into her mouth, moaning as she did so that the vibration rattled me to my core. I returned the attention by swiping up the center of her, pressing into the sensitive pearl and swirling my tongue around it. My arms clasped around her waist and held her in place as I lavished her with attention, and she made a playful groaning sound from around my cock. I kept myself busy, twirling my tongue around her, and feeling her legs beginning to tremble while she took my erection deep inside her mouth. Maddie continued to stroke me with one hand and massaged my balls with the other, and her moans increased in speed. Suddenly, she let out a cry and her body arched up, and I buried tongue in her, tasting her juices as she rode the wave of an orgasm.

CHAPTER 21

MADDIE

My body shook as the powerful orgasm took hold. When I finally felt like I had control of my legs again, I wiggled up so that I was sitting on his chest, continuing to stroke him, and I looked back over my shoulder. His eyes were open, and a knowing grin was stretched across his lips. He was aware of how strong I came, and that look was nearly daring me to return the favor. I bit my bottom lip, slid down his body, and rubbed my dripping pussy against the top of his cock. The groan that came from him told me that matching my orgasm wouldn't take long for him.

Sitting up on my knees, I rubbed the sensitive head through my folds, stroking him firmly and rocking my hips to tease him. I looked back again and saw his eyes clenched shut now, muscles tensed in his neck and chest as his hands wrapped around my hips. One hand reached down and cupped his balls, squeezing them gently, and then I sat down firmly on his cock.

Toby made a sound that was a mixture of surprise and pleasure, and I ground my hips down into his, letting him fill me with his girth. I placed my hands on his knees and lifted up a little before sliding back down, presenting my ass to him and letting him slide his hands to it and squeeze. A giggle bubbled up inside me as one hand smacked down on my butt, and I rocked on him, sliding him almost all the way out of me before coming back down. I settled into a rhythm and lay down further, letting my hips control the movement and forcing myself to focus completely on the feeling of him inside of me without visual stimulation.

His rock-hard cock seemed to thicken even more while in the grip of my wet core. I slid one hand down to massage his balls as I rocked into him again. My motion was slower now, more controlled, and I felt myself edging back, close to another loss of control. I increased the speed, and Toby's hands clenched on my hips, helping guide me in a harder, faster rhythm. I whimpered out as the depth of his cock buried inside me blurred the line between pain and pleasure.

Suddenly, Toby shifted below me, and I was pitched forward on the bed. A playful growl came from deep in his chest as he sat up, positioning himself on his knees and bringing me back to him by my hips. I flipped my hair out of the way and looked back at him hungrily. He pulled his hips forward and placed the head of his cock at my opening, and I ached for the moment when he would thrust into me. His hands gripped me tightly as he held me in place, dominating me with a confident power that made me melt. In this moment, I was his to do with what he pleased.

What he pleased was pulling me down hard on his cock so that my ass slammed into his hips. He held me there as I yelped out and grasped at the sheets. He waited a moment as I got used to the depth of the new position, and I arched my back, pushing my bottom into him further to let him know I was ready. His grip only grew tighter as he guided me, slowly at first, into a rhythm. Within moments, it ramped up in speed and intensity, and I couldn't stop myself from mumbling his name in a string of sounds. It only encouraged him, and he reached into my hair, grabbing a handful with one hand and pulling just tightly enough to increase the intensity.

I giggled and moaned in one sound, delighted by this new level of passion as his other hand slipped around me, a long, powerful pad of his middle finger reaching between my legs and finding my clit. His hips continued rocking into me, more of a thrust now, like he was trying to push himself as deeply as he could while his finger firmly pressed on my sensitive nub. I opened my mouth to yell out at the overwhelming sensation, but no sound came. I could only breathe, taking in the air and the smell of his musk as he drove me deeper into delirium. I knew I wouldn't be able to stop the orgasm coming with him so firmly in control, and instead bore down into it, experiencing it fully. My hips opened wide, and I clenched as the wave rolled over me.

My voice, which had abandoned me, now came back in full force, rising in pitch until I was nearly screaming in pleasure. The once playful grunts behind me grew deeper and more frantic. His cock was slamming into me faster, harder, and I knew he was near the brink as well. Knowing he was so close to ecstasy made me wetter, and I lost control of myself, writhing under his rapid thrusts and clenching hands. The fingers which had been exploring my center moved up and wrapped around one of my breasts, filling his palm with my nipple as he slowed down the speed, but increased the power of his strokes. The grunts rose in volume, and soon, he exploded into me, and our voices matched. He came deeply, with abandon, and I shook as he held me tightly in position. Sweat beaded down the small of my back, and he thrust again, emptying himself into me. I reached between my legs, finding the base of his cock and milking him until I felt him begin to crumple to the side.

I fell with him, and laughter bubbled up between us, a comfortable sound that filled my heart as much as he had filled my body. He curled into me, one arm wrapping around my waist and his hand cupping my breast as he exhaled deeply, chuckling, and I reached back to wrap my arm around his neck, doing the same.

The night with Toby in the gorgeous hotel helped me feel more confident the next day heading out onto the KU campus to find my sister. I knew the best place to look for her would be at the sorority house where she lived. Her entire life revolved around her sorority and the other girls in it. I didn't understand that. I'd never joined a sorority. I considered them expensive, frivolous wastes of time. It was still my perspective, even as my sister devoted herself totally to the organization she'd joined in the first few seconds she was on campus. For me, college had been about buckling down, keeping my nose to the grindstone, and making sure I got the best grades possible so I would appeal to a company after graduation.

My sister was different. Megan considered college an extended version of high school and, just like when she was actually in high school, had to be a part of the cool-girl clique.

We got to the house, and Toby and I walked inside. A girl seemed to appear out of nowhere in front of us. She had the presence of someone in charge, so I greeted her.

"I'd like to speak to Megan, please," I said.

At that moment a few other girls came bounding down

the steps. They heard me asking about my sister and shook their heads.

'Who are you?" the one who looked to be in charge asked.

"I'm her sister. Can you please tell her Maddie is here?"

"She isn't here," one told me.

"Is she in class?" I asked.

I hoped the incredulous note didn't show up in my voice. I didn't want them mentioning it to Megan and having her feel like I was being rude about her.

"No, she hasn't been staying here at the house much lately," another said.

"Where has she been?" I asked.

"She's been at her boyfriend's house off campus," the first girl told me.

I frowned, frustrated and upset by the news.

"Thank you," I told them and turned on my heel to leave the house, a mixture of fear and frustration welling up inside me.

"What happens next?" Toby asked. "We came all this way to talk to Megan and she isn't even here."

"I know exactly where to look. Come on," I said.

"Should we get the car?"

I shook my head. "No. It's not far. We can walk."

I'd done the walk countless times before. The half a mile took us only a few minutes before we arrived at a modest house. The overgrown lawn looked desolate and foreboding. I swallowed hard, tightening my hand around Toby's. Seeing the house was more uncomfortable than I thought it was going to be. I hadn't been there since I broke up with Craig, and the bad memories were still there, like they were waiting for me. But I wasn't going to let them chase me away. I wasn't going to back down. I needed to get my little sister the fuck out of there.

Taking a deep breath, I walked up the cracked sidewalk onto the steps and knocked on the door. It opened, but as soon as Megan saw me, she let out a yelp and slammed the door in my face. I started banging on it again.

"Megan, open up," I called. "Let me in."

A few seconds of increasingly aggressive smashing of my fists against the door convinced Megan to open it again, and she looked out at me with a sheepish expression.

"What are you doing here, Maddie?" she asked.

"You wouldn't take my calls," I reminded her. "So, now I'm here and you get to explain to my face why you're living in Craig's house. Even more importantly, you can explain to me why he has the crazy idea you're getting married."

Megan stepped out of the way and gestured for us to come in. She eyed Toby as he walked in after me.

"Who are you?" she asked.

I rolled my eyes. Megan was ever the welcoming hostess.

"It doesn't matter who he is. We're here to find out what you're up to," I told her.

Megan went into the kitchen, and I followed her, shuddering when I saw dirty dishes strewn across nearly every surface. I sighed as my sister pushed a few plates out of the way to make a space to sit at the table. She had never been one for housework, and neither had Craig. It looked like the combination was working out swimmingly. Toby and I sat down with her.

"Talk," I ordered.

"I ran into Craig on campus one day. We got to talking about where you were and what you were doing. He said he hadn't heard anything from you and didn't know what was going on. He seemed upset, so I tried to make him feel better. I told him how much I missed my big sister, too, and how I was doing bad because you weren't here to help me," Megan said.

"You've got to be kidding me," I muttered, struggling not to roll my eyes at the pity party unfolding in front of me.

"Craig told me he could help me, then asked me out to dinner. I went with him because he was being so nice to me. One thing led to another and... well, the next thing I knew we were dating." She looked at me almost desperately, leaning slightly across the table and looking at me with pouting eyes. "I never expected it to happen, Maddie. Really, I didn't."

"That's because I forbade it from happening. And I still do," I said flatly.

Megan frowned, her attitude shifting and a stormy look crossing her eyes.

"You're being ridiculous," Megan snapped at Maddie.

I was surprised by the blunt reaction. The way Maddie had described her sister, I was expecting far more of the pouting and for her to try to get her big sister to pity her rather than be angry with her. Part of me still suspected Megan was just trying to manipulate Maddie with the fake engagement. As soon as Maddie paid enough attention to her, she would reveal the ruse, and everything would go back to normal. But her reaction didn't fit with that.

"Excuse me?" Maddie asked. "*I'm* the one being ridiculous?"

"Yes," Megan said. "You forbid me to date someone? Who do you think you are? You don't make the rules, Maddie. Besides, even if you did, you haven't been around to enforce them. You ran off to do your own thing, not caring at all about what you were doing to me and to my life. Besides, Craig told me everything."

She crossed her arms over her chest, giving Maddie a

smug look. Maddie's eyes narrowed as she glared across the table at her little sister.

"What do you mean by that? What did he tell you?" Maddie asked.

"He told me all about the lies you've been spewing to everyone since the two of you broke up. He never did any of the things you said he did. He never did anything to you. I can't believe you would lie about such a good man. Especially about the types of things you said."

"Are you fucking serious right now, Megan?" Maddie fumed. "Are you seriously sitting there, not only defending the asshole who made my life a living nightmare I barely survived, but telling me I made it all up?"

"Yes," Megan said matter-of-factly. "At first, I didn't want to hear anything he had to say. I believed everything you said and thought he was the terrible person you made him out to be. Then I actually took the time to listen to him and let him give me his side of the story. And he told me the truth. That he never did anything to you and did everything he possibly could to make you happy. But you were cold and demanding and were never happy with anything. So, when he broke up with you, you came up with all these stories to try to make yourself look like the victim. You didn't want to look like the one who caused the problems and wanted to get your revenge on him. You threw around a bunch of lies so people would feel bad for you and you would look like some hero leaving town."

"That's bullshit, Megan, and you know it," Maddie seethed.

"The only thing full of shit around here is you," Megan snapped back. "I've been with Craig all this time, and he has never even gotten close to being the type of person you said he was. He has been a perfect gentleman with me. He treats me well, spoils me. He makes sure I have what I need and is wonderful to me. He does everything I need and gives me the kind of life I deserve. That's more than I can say for you."

Maddie glowered at Megan. "You're being a fool. Craig is just using you. He was nice to me at the beginning of our relationship, too. And with you he has even more reason to be on his best behavior for now. He's using you, little sister. He has no intention of marrying you."

Megan slammed her hands on the table and pushed herself up to standing so she could lean close to Maddie. Her eyes sparked, and her jaw was set so hard the muscles strained.

"You're just jealous!" she shouted. "You hate that he loves me, that he treats me well and I can make him happy in a way you never did. You've thought all this time you could just drag him along. You thought you could keep him tucked in your back pocket and pull him back out whenever you felt like it. All you've ever cared about is yourself and this big life you have planned in New York. That's why you dropped him the way you did. You didn't think he was good enough. You're so full of yourself you didn't think he'd be able to give you the life you want, and so you kicked him to the curb. Then you were enough of a raging bitch to lie about him so you could look like some brave and triumphant survivor when you left, rather than what you really are—a lying opportunist who will stomp on anyone's heart to get where you want to be."

"Wow. Opportunist. That's a big word for you," Maddie sneered.

"That's right, Maddie. Just go ahead and make fun of me. You can't stand that you don't have your backup anymore. You thought you could run off to New York for your big career, and if you fell on your ass, Craig would be there to act like your security net. Now you don't have that anymore, and it's driving you crazy. You hate that I'm the one who he wants now. Well, that's just tough shit. You had your chance, and you fucked it up. Craig is mine, and you have to accept it. You have no choice. You can't tell me what to do with my life. Get out of my house," Megan shouted, pointing angrily at the door.

Now it was Maddie's turn to stand and lean toward her sister, showing just as much aggression and anger. But hers was more intimidating. Rather than Megan's almost frantic shouting, Maddie's was even and simmering. It was the type of anger that could explode at any second. I'd already seen Maddie explode, and it wasn't something I thought Megan was prepared to handle. Something told me Maddie always did as much as she could to maintain her temper and not blow up on her little sister. But she was way beyond the point of wanting to protect Megan now.

"It isn't your house," she said. "It's Craig's. And you are the one who is going to get out. You are going to pack up and go back to the sorority house."

Megan laughed and pulled out her phone. It only rang briefly before I heard a muffled voice coming through. She cocked her hip, crossing her other arm over her stomach.

"Craig? Hey, babe. Maddie and some random guy are here at the house, and they're trying to make me leave," she said.

Her tone had a distinct whine to it, like a little girl complaining to an overindulgent parent that the other wants her to do her chores.

"What? Maddie and her husband?" Craig asked loudly enough for me to hear him clearly.

Megan's eyes widened, and she looked at Maddie, her

arm loosening from around her and her posture straightening.

"Did you get married and not tell me?" she asked, sounding somewhere between angry and hurt.

"Hang up the phone, Megan," Maddie told her.

"Answer my question. Did you get married and not even bother to tell your sister? Your only sister?"

"Megan, hang up the phone," Maddie said, lunging across the table to try to grab the phone out of her sister's hand.

"No. Tell me. Did you seriously just skip telling me he's your husband?" Megan asked.

Maddie walked around the side of the table and reached for the phone again. Megan slapped her hand away. She stepped backward and turned her back on Maddie, crunching slightly like she was trying to protect the phone from Maddie.

"Can you please come home now? I don't want you to be gone anymore," she said.

"Absolutely. I'll be on the next flight," Craig said.

Megan turned back around so we could see her face and smiled.

"Perfect. I love you, baby."

She made a few sickening kissy sounds into the phone, then hung up. Her arms crossed over her chest again, and she lowered a fierce glare at Maddie.

"You really need to get out. There's no point in you being here. You should just leave and go back to New York," she commanded.

"Think about it Megan. If I were really just wanting to have Craig for myself, would I have gone and married someone else?" Maddie asked, trying to get her sister to see reason.

Megan shrugged. "Honestly, I don't know Maddie. I don't know you at all anymore. Just go."

"I'm not going anywhere," Maddie said. "Not until I can talk some sense into you."

"Give it up, Maddie. I don't want you here, and you're not going to convince me of anything, so you need to just go back to your precious city and live the life you made for yourself there. Leave me alone to live mine."

"What is wrong with you?" Maddie asked.

"Wrong with me? Are you serious? You've changed and not for the better. How could you get married and not even tell me? How could you do that?" Megan asked.

Maddie stammered for a few seconds, then shook her head.

"We can talk about all of that once you're safely away from Craig. You aren't thinking clearly, Megan. You're being totally delusional. You need to go pack up your stuff and come with us back to the sorority house," Maddie insisted.

"No. I'm not going anywhere. I already told you that," Megan said.

I took a step forward, holding out a hand to try to defuse the situation as much as I could.

"Craig isn't even here. He's still in New York and probably isn't going to be able to get a flight until tomorrow at the earliest. Why don't you just go back to the sorority house until he's back, or even just for the night, to make your sister feel better?" I suggested.

Megan looked me up and down, then shifted her weight so she leaned slightly toward me.

"Why would you marry my sister in secret? Because I know damn well Craig didn't just make that up," she said.

"We work together and that creates a somewhat delicate situation, so we haven't told anyone yet—"

"None of that matters," Maddie snapped, cutting me off. "I'm not the one with the problem right now. Megan, I'm worried about you, and you're obviously not thinking clearly. I need you to pack up and come with me. I know what's best for you."

Megan's face reddened, and her eyes flashed with fury.

"Get out! Get out now or I'm calling the police and telling them I have two intruders in my home attempting to remove me against my will. You abandoned me, Maddie. You aren't allowed to tell me what to do anymore," she shouted.

This wasn't going to have a good resolution. That was very obvious. Getting the two of them away from each other was going to be the best thing I could do. I reached down for Maddie's hand and led her out the door. As soon as we stepped outside, Megan slammed the door behind us. Maddie flinched at the loud sound bursting in the air around us, then threw her hands up in despair.

"How could she be like that? What am I supposed to do now?" she asked.

I wrapped my arm around her shoulders and squeezed her close, leaning down to press a kiss into her hair.

"Come on. Let's just go before she calls the police and makes things worse. We'll figure something out."

CHAPTER 23

MADDIE

I couldn't sleep. Even with Toby lying beside me, his body warm and comforting, I couldn't make myself settle down enough to actually get any rest. My brain wouldn't stop spinning, my thoughts refusing to quiet down as I struggled to make sense of anything happening around me. I was so upset about Megan. I couldn't even put it into words. When we got back from the showdown at Craig's house, Toby ordered room service and sat beside me on the couch, letting me know he was there for me. If I wanted to talk, he would listen. If I needed to scream and vent, he would sit there and let me do it. If I needed to ramble and try to unravel the whole thing so it somehow made sense, he would sit with me and help me through in whatever way he could.

But it didn't do any good. I tried to talk, but the words died in my throat before they came out. It wasn't that I didn't want to share with Toby, or that I didn't trust him. I opened up to him completely and appreciated his willingness to go through this whole thing with me. I was just so upset I couldn't untangle it. I didn't know what to do next. When Toby fell asleep beside me, I lay there trying to rest, hoping if I could just get some rest, everything would seem clearer when the morning came. Only the morning came and not only was I tired, but nothing seemed clearer.

It was barely after dawn when I finally gave up. There was no point in staying in bed anymore. I got up and dressed as quietly as I could so I didn't wake Toby up, then snuck out of the room. It was chilly as I walked to the diner I used to eat in all the time when I was in college. It was a favorite spot of mine, a hidden little gem most of the students didn't go to because it was further out from campus than the rest of the restaurants they frequented.

The diner was fairly empty because it was still so early, it was even before the breakfast rush. As soon as I walked in, the memories of all the long days and nights I spent in that diner came rushing back. This was where I crammed for my tests and suffered over every word of term papers. It was where I hid away from the chaos of campus so I could focus and not have to deal with every-thing else. All the time I spent there made the diner like a second home and created familiarity and habits. Those came back as I stepped inside and went directly to the booth in the back corner. It was the booth I'd come to know as "mine." It saw me through years of classwork, extra projects, applications, resumes, and tears. Not all of the tears had to do with that stress. The diner is where I would also come to hide away from the pain of Craig when things were bad, and I hadn't yet gotten away from him.

In a way, that's what I was doing again. I was going back to where I felt safe and the space that helped me so much when I needed it before. Almost as soon as I sat down, a waitress walked up to the side of the table. I smiled up at her, and her eyes widened.

"Maddie?" she asked, surprised to see me there after a few years.

"Hi, Wanda," I said. "It's good to see you. How have you been?"

"I've been good. Had a new baby since you've been here," she told me.

"That's wonderful news. Congratulations," I said.

"And how about you?" she asked. "What have you been up to? You look..."

Her voice trailed off as her eyes searched my face. She had that look on her face people get when they've talked their way into a corner and are trying to figure out how to get out of it. I gave a mirthless laugh to ease her discomfort.

"Exhausted? Stressed? Like ever-loving shit? You go ahead and choose the adjective," I said.

Wanda smiled. "Well, I'll agree with the first two. You're just as beautiful as ever, though. I heard you went to New York."

"I did. I work in the marketing department of a technology and software development firm," I told her.

"And there you go. How do you expect to feel anything but stress and exhaustion when you're doing something like that every day?" she asked. "It's a good thing you're home. You'll get some rest and feel much better. Now, what can I get you? Coffee?"

"Definitely. And the breakfast special," I ordered.

"Be right to you."

She stepped away for a second to get a mug, brought it back to the table, and filled it with steaming hot coffee. I smiled at her and took a sip as she walked away. If only the exhaustion and stress on my face were really caused by my job. That would be so much easier to handle than what I was actually going through. I nursed the mug of coffee as I considered what to do next. Obviously, my sister wasn't interested in hearing my opinion about Craig. Clearly, she thought she knew best and wasn't going to let me persuade her at all. Even though, of all people, I knew what she was facing. I knew what was best for her and what she was getting herself into. Megan wasn't listening to me. She wasn't even open to hearing me out.

The worst part was Craig was conning her. He didn't love her. This wasn't a situation of them falling in inconvenient love and me railing against it because of some sort of lingering feelings of possession. This wasn't even him trying to prove himself as a changed man and me refusing to accept the possibility. Craig didn't want a relationship with Megan because of Megan; it was all a ploy. He was using my little sister as leverage to force my hand. Would I really go back to him to keep him from hurting Megan? I couldn't believe I was faced with that choice.

Wanda came back to the table and put two plates in front of me. Overflowing with eggs, bacon, sausage, toast, grits, and fruit, it was the same breakfast I ate countless times before. Definitely not the healthiest option, and I was probably going to have to do penance at the office gym when I got back to New York, but it was worth it. As I ate my breakfast and aimlessly flipped through my phone, I noticed someone slide into the booth across from me. Thinking it might be Toby, but not knowing how he would know where I was, I looked up. As soon as I did, my fork fell from my hand.

"What the hell are you doing here?" I asked Craig, keeping my voice low as to not call the attention of the other people in the diner. "When Megan talked to you yesterday, you were still in New York."

"Good morning, Maddie. Funny to find you here. Actually, it's not at all. You're completely predictable. I caught the red-eye back as soon as I found out you came to confront Megan, and I knew you'd end up dragging yourself in here. You just can't resist the siren song of a greasy spoon, can you?" he asked.

"Why are you doing this, Craig? We broke up years ago. It's over. It's *been* over. Why are you insisting on inserting yourself back into my life?"

"For me, it wasn't over. You made that decision all on your own. You had no right to leave me. You're mine. You were mine then, and you're still mine. The sooner you realize it, the sooner all this can stop. I will leave Megan alone. All you have to do is come home and be with me. No more of this nonsense. No more of you living off in New York like you think you're someone you're not. Come back home where you belong, and we can have a life we were always supposed to have. And your little sister can go on with her own life and won't have to be a part of any of this anymore."

I couldn't believe what I was hearing. Craig was sitting there in the diner, dangling my sister's future, and mine, in front of me. He seriously believed he could convince me to just throw everything away and come back to him. I had to give it to him, it was a compelling argument. He was using the thing he knew was most important to me as some twisted form of currency. But I wasn't going to rise to the bait.

"No, Craig. I'm not going to rearrange my life to suit you. I don't love you, and I'm never going to be with you again."

He looked at me with a slight, almost cruel smirk on his face. Taking a piece of toast from my plate, he bit off the corner, then looked me in the eyes.

"Are you willing to sacrifice Megan? Because your little sister *will* marry me. And I can promise you I won't treat her nearly as well as I treated you." He took another bite of the toast. "So you'd better be sure about your choice."

I instantly felt sick to my stomach. Bile rose up in my throat, and I knew I couldn't stand to be in the same space with him for another minute. Standing up sharply, I threw down a handful of cash in the middle of the table, then quickly walked out the door without another word. But he wasn't giving up that easily. Craig got up and followed right behind me.

"Don't you dare walk away from me," he yelled angrily out on the sidewalk. "Who the hell do you think you are walking away from me?"

I didn't turn around, but he caught up with me and grabbed my arm. He yanked me around so hard it hurt, and I cried out. Stunned he would put his hands on me now after everything, I couldn't hold back the rage that rose up in me. I slapped him hard across the face.

"Get your hands off me. Don't you fucking touch me," I told him.

Craig didn't let me go. Instead, he tightened his grip on my arm and used it to drag me across the sidewalk and closer to the street. The morning traffic was picking up, and cars rolled past without paying attention to what was happening just feet away. I struggled and fought against Craig's grip, but he didn't relent, and I wasn't strong enough to break free. No one seemed to notice what was happening, even when I shouted at him to let me go. He pulled me up against him hard, bringing his face so close to mine his nose touched mine.

"If I can't have you, Maddie, no one is going to," he growled.

"Get off me," I told him.

He drew in a breath between his teeth, cracking his neck from side to side. His eyes locked on mine again, and I could see the wild fury in them.

"This is your last chance. Either you come home to me, or you're going to pay," he said.

I struggled harder, trying to free myself. He'd pushed me to the very edge of the sidewalk, and I was balanced on the curb, trying to stay in place. No matter how hard I fought, his grip was like a vise. But I wasn't going to give into him. He didn't have that power over me anymore.

"Go fuck yourself," I told him through gritted teeth.

He shook his head like he wasn't going to accept the words. His grip lessened just slightly, and I pulled again. Suddenly, Craig let go. The abrupt release of tension sent me stumbling off the edge of the curb and into the street. I tumbled to the ground and skidded across the pavement. My head smacked into the hard asphalt, and I was too dazed to move before hearing the screech of tires. Everything went black, and the world exploded in pain.

CHAPTER 24

For the second time in as many days, I didn't know where Maddie was. This was becoming a habit I really didn't appreciate, and I planned on having a talk with her about it as soon as I figured out where she'd gone off to. I really didn't like waking up without her beside me. After all the stress and conflict of the day before, I wanted Maddie to take some time to relax. She deserved to enjoy the luxurious surroundings of the hotel, maybe order some room service for breakfast and soak away all her tension in the sunken tub. I knew she wasn't going to just give up and head back to the city. Not yet, at least. There was going to be another confrontation with Megan, and I wanted to give Maddie some grace before that happened.

Waking up to a cold bed and an empty hotel room meant my plans were foiled. At first, I told myself she was just getting some fresh air. Maybe she had gone for a walk to clear her mind and think everything through on her own. I didn't love the idea of her being out by herself, but she was a grown woman. And, after all, this was her hometown. She knew it better than she knew anywhere else, and it had been so long since she was here, she may have gotten a flash of nostalgia. I gave it some time. But she never showed back up. After a while, I started calling her. But there was no answer.

I kept calling, kept texting. Eventually, her voice mailbox was full, and I couldn't leave any more messages. I still hadn't heard from her and was getting worried. Wanting to see her as soon as she got back, I paced back and forth across the hotel lobby. Every time the door opened, I looked up, hoping it was Maddie. But she never arrived. Three hours passed.

Finally, I couldn't take it anymore. I had to go look for her. I got dressed and headed out of the hotel, first taking a quick walk around the block and then the surrounding neighborhood just to make sure she hadn't gone for a morning stroll and been distracted by an old neighbor. I didn't want to overreact or seem like I was even getting close to turning into the same type of controlling monster Craig was. But when I got back to the front of the hotel, my worry had reached an even higher peak. There was no sign of Maddie.

There was only one more place to look for her. Waiting for the valet to get the rental car would take too long. Instead, I took off running in the direction of Craig's house. I stomped up the side and walked onto the front porch, pounding on the door until Megan opened it. She stared out at me, her eyes searching around me like they were trying to find her sister.

"What are you doing here?" Megan asked, obviously not pleased to find me standing on her porch.

"I'm looking for Maddie," I told her. "Is she here?"

Megan shook her head, dropping her hip and pulling

the door so it was almost in front of her. It was a defensive move, like she was readying herself for me storming into the house.

"No. I haven't seen her today. You better get out of here before Craig gets back."

It was obvious I wasn't going to get any more information from Megan. As much as I didn't have a good sense of who she was and had gotten some impression of her unreliability from Maddie, she didn't seem to be lying. I believed she hadn't seen her sister, which meant Maddie was still out there somewhere and I needed to find her. Every minute that passed made me more worried and gave me more of a fear that something terrible had happened. I started back down the steps but turned to face Megan again before leaving.

"You know, Megan, Maddie is the most trustworthy person I know. The most trustworthy person I have *ever* known. If she says Craig abused her, he did. You should heed the warning and be careful," I told her in a serious tone.

Megan only shrugged. "Maddie was always jealous of the attention I got. She's been that way our whole lives. It's just part of who she is. I know my sister better than you do."

"I know her very well," I argued. "I know her in a different way than you do."

Before I could continue, Megan's phone rang. She didn't even bother to feign embarrassment at turning her attention away from the conversation we were having and reaching for her phone. She picked it up and answered it in the middle of my sentence. I watched her expression, trying to determine who she was talking to and assuming it was Craig. But she didn't greet the caller like she had greeted Craig when I heard their conversation the day before. Instead, she barely got out a hello before her face fell.

"Yes, this is Megan." She paused and listened. "Yes, she's my sister."

That perked up my attention, and I took a step closer to her.

"Who is that? What's going on?" I asked.

Megan held up a hand, waving me off to silence me. Her eyes widened in shock, and a jolt of worry rushed up through me.

"I'll be right there," she said.

She hung up and shoved the phone in her pocket.

"What's going on?" I demanded.

"Maddie is in the hospital," she said. "I'm still listed as her emergency contact, so they called me."

"What happened?" I asked, feeling frantic.

I should have looked for her sooner. I shouldn't have stayed at the hotel and waited around for so long. She was in danger, and I wasn't there to protect her or take care of her.

"I don't know," Megan said. "They couldn't tell me over the phone. They just said that I needed to get up to the hospital as soon as possible."

She looked understandably upset and worried, so I took a step closer, looking directly into her face to make her focus on me.

"We need to get there right now. Do you have a car?" I asked.

She shook her head. "No. Totaled mine a couple of years ago and never replaced it. I live on campus, so I didn't really see the point. Besides, I wasn't ever able to save up the money."

She was babbling, startled and worried into not being

able to control the words coming out of her mouth. I groaned in frustration, wishing I'd bothered to get the rental car out of the hotel parking deck. There wasn't time to go back there now. Instead, I opened my phone and used a rideshare app to order a car to pick us up. My stomach was in my throat. The thought of Maddie hurt made me feel sick and on the edge of my control. What could have happened to her?

It seemed like far too long, but it was really only a few minutes before the car pulled up. I immediately opened the door and climbed into the back seat. Megan didn't move away from the sidewalk. I gestured to her.

"Come on. Get in and we can get to the hospital," I said.

She hesitated. "I need to call Craig."

Infuriated that thought would even go through her mind at this moment, I slammed the door and told the driver to go. The entire ride to the hospital was full of anxiety. My stomach twisted and turned; my heart pounded in my chest and my head felt hot, like it was going to explode at any second. I hated that Megan was the one the hospital called when Maddie was in trouble. I understood it. Megan was her little sister and the only family she had. It would make sense she would be the one on the emergency contact for the hospital, but it felt isolating not being the one to get to the information. If I hadn't been standing there with her when she got the phone call, Megan probably wouldn't have even told me what was going on. Her first instinct was to call Craig and tell him, so I wouldn't have even crossed her mind. There would have been no way of knowing Maddie was in trouble, and I would have just kept fuming and trying to figure out what was going on. It was a sickening thought.

I wished I had more details. Anything to let me know what had happened or if she was all right. But they couldn't release that type of information over the phone, and certainly wouldn't tell me. I had the door to the car open before it even got all the way out to the curb. I jumped out and ran into the emergency room. The woman behind the desk looked at me with startled eyes when I slammed my hands on the counter and asked for Maddie.

"Are you family?" she asked. "Only family is able to see her now."

"I'm her husband," I said.

She gave a nod and slid back away from the desk. "I'll take you back. I'm sorry I didn't call you. Her sister was the one listed in her file."

"We just got married, and we live in New York," I explained, thankful for the story to fall back on. Without it, they would have left me in the waiting room without any idea what was going on until Megan finally made her way to the hospital, if she ever ended up there at all.

We got to an examination room, and the woman opened the door to let me look inside. I saw Maddie lying in a hospital bed, her eyes closed. Bruises and scrapes covered every bit of skin I could see. It was devastating seeing her that way. I wanted to run to her and gather up into my arms. I didn't ever want to let her go or have her out of my sight again, but before I was able to even get to her bedside, a nurse came in.

"We've had her under observation since she came in. Now that we're confident she's stable, the doctor has ordered a series of tests. After those, we'll be admitting her. She'll be moved up to a room outside in the emergency area. You can visit with her there," the nurse said.

"Where are they moving her?" I asked.

"She hasn't been assigned to a specific room, yet. If you'll go to the waiting room, we'll have more information to you as soon as it's available."

"I want to stay with her," I told her. "I'm her husband."

"I'm sorry," the nurse said. "It's not allowed. No one can be with her during these tests. I assure you, as soon as we have some answers and you are able to be with her, someone will come to get you. Now, come with me and I'll bring you back to the waiting area."

She escorted me back through the emergency department and out to the rows of blue fake leather chairs. She stayed close behind me like she thought at any second I was going to break away from her and run back to Maddie. It was a fair assessment.

I dropped down into one of the chairs and stared at the TV bolted to the wall. The volume was so low I could only just hear any sound coming from it. They weren't enough to follow the show playing, and soon I couldn't sit there anymore. I got up and started pacing, stewing as I worried about Maddie. The feeling of helplessness pushed me close to cracking as every possible scenario went through my head, and I longed to be near her.

CHAPTER 25

I woke up feeling foggy, like my head was stuffed with cotton, and I couldn't force cohesive thoughts through my brain. I had no idea what had happened. I didn't even know where I was. The last thing I remembered was talking to Wanda and then eating my breakfast at the diner. When I opened my eyes, an unfamiliar face was staring down at me. It took me a second to process the image and realize the woman was wearing a white coat and had a stethoscope draped around her neck. She was a doctor, which meant the bright light and cold room, sharp with the smell of disinfectant hand gel, was a hospital. That didn't make any sense. I was at the diner, and then I was walking down the sidewalk. How did I end up in the hospital?

"What happened?" I croaked.

I started to try to sit up, but pain flickered through my body, and dizziness made me lie back down. The doctor put her hand on my shoulder and guided me back, patting me as if to say I shouldn't be moving that much. I didn't really need the encouragement. The way my head was spinning and the ache through virtually every part of my body was enough to keep me in laying down for as long as she wanted.

"I'm Dr. Barnes, Maddie. I've been taking care of you since the ambulance brought you into the emergency room," the doctor said.

"I'm in the emergency room?" I asked, turning my head just enough to look at the room around me.

"No. Not anymore. We performed a series of tests on you and moved you into another unit," she told me.

"Why am I here?" I asked.

"You were hit by a car on the street. Do you remember anything?"

Hit by a car? It sounded preposterous. I tried to think back, to remember anything after drinking my coffee and digging into the eggs on my plate. But there was nothing. I shook my head, which caused a series of small explosions rocketing through my skull.

"No. I don't remember anything happening," I told Dr. Barnes.

"That's all right. You might remember more later. For right now, all that matters is the driver called for emergency medical services as soon as it happened and you were able to get here when you did. Fortunately, your injuries aren't life-threatening as far as I've been able to tell. I'm still waiting for all the test results to come back to make sure there isn't anything else serious going on, and there isn't any internal bleeding. But I feel confident you are extremely lucky and are just going to have to deal with some bumps and bruises for a while. How is your pain level?" she asked.

"Pretty bad," I admitted. "Especially my hip, and my head is hurting."

The longer I was awake, the more intense the pain pulsing behind my eyes and searing down the back of my neck became. The doctor nodded and peeked through my chart briefly.

"I can definitely understand that. People don't say they feel like they got hit by a truck when they're having a bad time for no reason." She gave a short laugh. "It might not have been a truck, but even a compact car can do some damage when it's coming at you at that speed. I've only given you acetaminophen as of right now, because I wanted to talk to you about the options before I administered or prescribed anything more serious."

"The options?" I asked, feeling confused, like I was missing something.

"Yes. Fortunately, the availability of acceptable medication has increased substantially, but it's important to me that we take the time to go over the different options, their risks and benefits, and compare them with any notes you've gotten from your doctor so you can make an informed decision," she said.

"I'm sorry," I said, shaking my head, "I think I'm still trying to get my head to work. I'm not following you."

Dr. Barnes gave a kind smile. "You're going to need painkillers for at least the next few days to help you cope with your injuries. They are serious, but they will be painful and you're going to be sore and stiff for a while. But we'll have to use a particular kind that is safe for the baby."

Now I knew my brain wasn't working correctly. There was no way I'd heard that correctly. Baby? Did she seriously just say baby?

"What do you mean?" I asked.

"You didn't know," she said. It wasn't a question, but a resigned statement. "I was afraid that was going to be the case."

"You were afraid what was going to be the case?" I asked, absolutely nothing making sense at the moment.

I heard her and knew what she'd said, but it still wasn't fully processing. I needed to hear it again, just to make sure.

"It is customary to give every woman of childbearing age a pregnancy test when they come into the emergency room. This is especially important for women who are unconscious or otherwise unable to effectively communicate. Pregnancy alters the types of tests and treatments that are safe for the woman, so it's one of the first things I want to know about my patients. When your test came back positive, I performed a cursory ultrasound to check how far along you are and to make sure the baby wasn't compromised in the accident," she said.

There was something about the clinical way she said "compromised" that made my heart clench. It was all so much. I just found out I'd been hit by a car even though I couldn't remember anything, yet the only thing I was thinking about in that moment was whether the injuries to my own body caused even worse ones to the tiny baby I hadn't even known existed.

"What did you find?" I managed to ask.

"The fetus looks good. You're not very far along, just a few weeks. Everything is just fine and developing well, but we have to be very careful about your treatment. The early weeks are the most delicate, and the chances of compromising the fetus's health are the highest."

I held up my hand to stop her, wincing slightly. "Can we find a different word to use, please?"

Dr. Barnes gave a slight smile.

"What matters is your baby looks good, and we just want to make sure anything you take is safe. We'll keep you overnight for observation, but I should be able to let you go home tomorrow. Congratulations, by the way."

She smiled a little bigger and patted my leg before walking out of the room. I sat there alone, my mind reeling. I was hit by a car? And I was pregnant? Maybe it wasn't real. Maybe it was all just a bad dream. But as soon as that thought went through my head, the door opened again, and Toby looked in. His eyes filled with worry when he saw me, and he rushed to the side of the bed, picking up my hand and kissing it.

"Oh, Maddie. What happened?" he asked.

I shook my head. "I don't remember. I woke up here and have no idea what happened. The doctor said I was hit by a car, but I don't remember that."

"Let's try to figure it out. Retrace your day," he said. He pulled a chair close to the edge of the bed and sat down, still holding my hand in both of his. "You weren't in bed with me when I woke up. When did you get up? Where did you go?"

I thought about it for a few seconds, piecing together the first hours of the day.

"I couldn't sleep," I told him. "After everything that happened with Megan, I just couldn't get myself to relax. I got up really early and walked down to the diner I used to go to when I was in college. I didn't want to wake you up, so I figured I would get some coffee, maybe some breakfast. Just take some time to think and see if any brilliant ideas came to mind."

As I was talking, a flash suddenly came into my mind. An image of a hand grabbing a piece of toast from my plate. The memory of Craig appearing at the diner and what happened after crashed over me, and I suddenly felt like it was harder to breathe. My hand tightened around Toby's, and I pressed the other to the center of my chest. I could feel Craig's hand around my arm again, and all around me I heard the sound of the tires squealing and people screaming.

"Maddie? What is it? What's wrong?" Toby asked.

"I can't believe it," I murmured.

"What do you mean? You can't believe what?" he asked.

"I was at the diner eating breakfast, and Craig showed up. He got a red eye last night when he found out I was here. He told me either I needed to come back to Kansas and be with him, or he was going to marry Megan. He implied he would be really horrible to her, that he would make her life even worse than he made mine," I told him.

Toby's expression hardened, and I could see the anger growing in his eyes.

"What did you say?" he asked.

"I told him no, of course," I said. "I said I wasn't going to come back here, that I don't love him, and we weren't going to be together again, ever. Then I got up to leave. I was intending on going back to the hotel, but he followed me. He grabbed me and pushed me until I was standing on the very edge of the curb, barely able to keep my balance. I tried to get away from him, but he was holding me too tightly and I couldn't. He said if he couldn't have me, no one would, and when I said I wasn't coming back, he let go of my arm and let me fall into traffic. Then I woke up here."

Toby was livid. He got to his feet and started pacing back and forth across the hospital room with long, purposeful strides.

"He didn't let you fall into traffic. He fucking pushed you in front of that car. I'm going to find that asshole and kill him," he said.

"Toby, please calm down."

His intensity was scaring me. I'd never seen him this way.

"I'm not going to stand for this, Maddie. This time, Craig is going to pay."

"Please. Please, Toby, sit down," I begged. "Too much has happened already. I can't watch you go to jail because of it, too."

He sat back down, but the tension had him shaking. His legs bounced and his jaw twitched.

"What did the doctor say?" he finally asked.

"They're going to keep me for observation overnight, but I should be okay and will be able to go home tomorrow," I told him.

For a moment, I considered telling him what the doctor had said about the pregnancy but decided against it. There was no point in me adding one more thing to our already very full plates. There was so much uncertainty around everything just then and adding a baby to the mix would only add to the chaos. Not to mention, Toby had only offered to pretend to be my husband to help me scare Craig off. He hadn't said anything about wanting to be together for real, and certainly nothing about a baby. No. I would have to wait until things calmed down and find a way to deal with the information then. Right then, my biggest concern was getting my sister away from Craig.

The nurse came in and adjusted my IV. Within seconds, I felt very sleepy and realized the doctor must have ordered the medication she'd mentioned. It didn't take long for me to drift off to sleep.

The medication the nurse put into Maddie's IV affected her quickly, and I watched her fall asleep. When she did, I didn't waste any time. As soon as she looked peaceful, I took out my phone and called my lawyer.

"Blake, it's Toby. I have kind of an urgent question to ask you," I said.

"Hey, Toby. Good to hear from you. What's going on? Nothing serious, I hope."

He laughed, but I couldn't join him in it.

"Actually, it is. I need to know if I can get a restraining order against someone on my wife's behalf," I said.

There was silence on the other end of the phone, and I knew the attorney I'd been working with since the company started to get successful was trying to figure out if I was playing some sort of odd joke on him. After a few seconds, he cleared his throat.

"First of all, I didn't know you were married. That's something I figured I would have known about. Do we need to have a conversation about the importance of a prenuptial agreement when there's a matter of significant wealth?" he asked.

"Now is not the time for that. Besides, I'm not exactly married. Not yet, anyway. But I might as well be."

I realized as I said it, but in my mind, I already considered Maddie my wife. She was everything to me; there was no way the part of my world she filled was ever going to be the same. I loved her with all of my being, more than I ever could have imagined. That part of me, that part of my life, was made for her, and I wasn't about to let her go. I also wasn't about to let some jackass with a God complex put her at risk or make her uncomfortable.

"So, you aren't legally married?" Blake asked.

"No. Not legally," I said. "But the situation is extremely serious, and she needs protection as soon as possible. Her ex-boyfriend has verbally threatened her life, and it has now escalated into a physical assault. Something needs to be done to make sure she stays safe. I realize a restraining order isn't exactly a bulletproof shield or anything, but it's a start."

"I understand your concern, Toby. Really, I do. And I'm extremely sorry she's having to go through this and that you're having to watch her go through it. Unfortunately, because you aren't married legally, you don't have the ability to make those types of decisions for her. You have no legal stance and can't interfere with what is technically her personal business. Because she is an adult and can determine who she is in a relationship with and how she will engage with that person, she has to make the decision to get a restraining order, then go through the process of filing it on her own," Blake said.

"She's in the hospital right now, because of him. He pushed her in front of a car, and she got hit. She is under medication," I said, trying to get him to understand the severity of the situation. "There has to be something that can be done. Some measure that can be put into place to protect her, or at least make it easier to take him down if he does try to get to her again."

"Again, Toby, I understand where you're coming from. This is an awful situation, and I wish you didn't have to go through it. If there was something I could do, I would. But she's an adult and has no legal ties to you. There's nothing you can do. She has to file it for herself. Good luck."

I looked down at Maddie again, making sure she was still asleep. She looked comfortable, but the bruises and scrapes on her skin stood out, making my blood boil. I touched my fingertips gently to a patch of purple discoloration along her cheekbone and felt my hand shaking. Heading out to the nurse's station, I asked how long the medication would keep her asleep. I didn't want her to wake up and be alone. The nurse assured me the doctor sedated her enough to keep her asleep for several hours in order to help her body heal. That would be plenty of time.

Thanking the nurse, I assured her I would be back well before that and stormed out of the hospital. Another rideshare appeared within minutes, and I got in the back seat. We were pulling out of the hospital parking lot when my phone rang. It was Nik.

"Hey," I said, not feeling up to much more of a greeting than that.

"So, Blake just called me," he said.

"He did?" I asked.

"Yep. Care to enlighten me about what exactly is going on and why you would need a restraining order for the wife you don't have?" Nik asked.

I let out an exasperated, angry breath. This definitely

wasn't something I wanted to get into with anyone right then, but hearing Nik's voice made me realize I needed to let out some steam. If there was anyone else in the world I trusted other than Maddie, it was Nik. Especially considering how his relationship with his own wife started, he would be the one most likely to commiserate with me. Very aware of the driver right in front of me, listening to everything I was saying, but not caring, I launched into an explanation of everything that had happened. It took the majority of the drive, but I told him everything. When I was finally finished, Nik sat in silence, obviously shocked.

"Well, that makes things a little clearer," he finally said. "At least you had the presence of mind to be asking about getting a restraining order against Craig, rather than one for Craig against you, which might be the more pressing need right at this moment in time. And just to be clear, you can't kill the fucker. Though, I don't blame you if you want to."

"Oh, I definitely want to. I'm on my way to his house right now," I told him.

"That's probably not the best idea. You don't want to make the situation worse by ending up in jail," Nik pointed out.

"That's exactly what Maddie said," I grumbled.

"And probably with good reason," he continued. "But you're not going to go that route. Instead, we're going to call some of our superior resources into play."

"What do you mean?"

"Just leave that to me. I'm going to make some calls. You should go back to the hospital and be with Maddie. She needs you now. Leave Craig to me," he said.

I hung up but wasn't completely satisfied with Nik's advice. I liked the sound of him bringing in some of his resources, knowing this could go beyond just destroying

Craig in the immediate moment. Nik's tremendous network of connections could allow far more extensive complications. But that wasn't enough. Not now. I couldn't just sit around in the hospital while Maddie slept and let Craig go about his life as if nothing happened. I was going to find the fucker and smash his face in. After that, I'd find out what more Nik could do, and we'd go from there. I was sure his connections could also solve the little complication of me getting arrested. A night in jail would be well worth causing Craig some serious pain. I knew it wouldn't even be a fraction of what he'd done to Maddie. Not now and not in their relationship, but it was a starting point.

The car pulled up in front of Craig's house, and I told the driver not to wait. Slamming the door, I stalked onto the porch, beating on the door so hard it sent shudders up my arm. When it opened, it wasn't Craig looking back at me. It was Megan again. She looked at me like she was expecting me to rip her to shreds over not coming to the hospital to be with her sister. In all honesty, I wanted to, but I was holding that conversation in reserve. My priority was Craig.

"I'm looking for Craig. Where is he?" I demanded.

"I don't know," she said. She looked worried and shifted her weight back and forth on her feet. "He isn't answering his calls. He must be on the plane."

I rolled my eyes and scoffed at her incredible naivete.

"He isn't on a plane," I told her, saying each word slowly to make sure she fully followed what I was saying to her. "He's already here."

"What?" she asked as if she didn't completely hear me.

"He's here already," I told her again.

"When did he get in?" Megan asked.

"Early enough to find Maddie at the diner where she

was eating breakfast and shove her into oncoming traffic," I spat.

Megan shook her head adamantly. "You must be crazy. He wouldn't do anything like that."

"I'm not. And yes, he absolutely would. Maddie, your big sister, is in a hospital bed, bruised and bleeding, because of what that asshole did to her. I know you can't possibly be stupid enough to not know he's here, or to think you can convince me you don't. Tell me where he is."

"I don't know. I swear. I didn't know he was back," Megan pleaded. She started crying, her eyes filled with genuine fear. "Is Maddie really hurt?"

I immediately felt bad for the way I spoke to her. As upset and afraid as I was, I had to remember that Megan was another one of Craig's victims. She didn't realize it, and the situation hadn't gotten bad yet, but she was most certainly being manipulated by him. I had to show her some compassion. My anger deflated, and I stepped up closer to put my arm around her.

"Yes," I told her. "She really is hurt. And the doctor is keeping her overnight for observation and has her pretty heavily medicated right now. But we're going to go up to the hospital and wait for her to wake up. You need to talk to your sister."

CHAPTER 27

MADDIE

I didn't know how long I was asleep, but I didn't feel as foggy coming out of it as I did the first time. There was definitely still some pain throughout my body, but whatever medication the doctor gave me was working well and I was able to relax. When I opened my eyes, I expected to see Toby still sitting there beside the bed. What I wasn't expecting was who was there in the room with him. Megan stood at the end of the bed, staring down at me as she held herself around the waist with one arm and chewed on the end of her other thumb. It was a habit she'd had from the time she was a little girl. Anytime she was feeling particularly anxious or upset about something, she would chew on it.

"I thought you grew out of that," I commented, nodding slightly toward her hand.

Her thumb fell out of her mouth, and she looked down at it. Tears welled up in her eyes.

"How are you feeling?" she asked.

It seemed like a fairly ridiculous question considering

the circumstances, but I also couldn't think of much else to introduce the conversation and get us talking. I tried to adjust my position so I could sit up, but a new surge of pain and a wave of dizziness kept me down.

"Well, I guess I feel like I got hit by a truck. A car, technically. But I'm okay," I told her.

I didn't know why I was trying to make her feel better. If there was anyone other than Craig who should not only not feel better about what was going on, but should probably feel like absolute shit about it, that would be Megan. Not that it was her fault what Craig was doing to her, but it was most certainly her fault how she was choosing to react to it. God, here I was, doing everything I could to comfort her and try not to let my little sister get too upset. It was the same role I'd been playing for so many years.

"Is it true?" Megan asked. "Is what Toby told me true? Did Craig do this?"

I drew in a breath and let it out slowly.

"Yes," I told her. "He did."

"Was it an accident?"

I tried not to let the question make me angry. I couldn't really blame her for asking it. Nobody would want to think the man they were engaged to would be capable of doing something like this to anybody, much less their own sister.

"No," I said flatly. "It was not an accident. Craig did this intentionally. He told me he would leave you alone if I moved back in with him."

Megan immediately broke down in tears. Her body shook with sobs, and she covered her face with both hands. It took several seconds for her to be able to get a hold of herself enough to talk to me again.

"I'm sorry. I'm so sorry, Maddie. I can't believe this is

happening. I don't love Craig. I never did. I just wanted you to pay attention to me. I've missed you so much, and things are so different without you here. I feel like you're not even a part of my life anymore, and it hurt so much. I just wanted you to notice me and to be like my big sister again. Like we used to be. I never should have done this," she sobbed.

"I'm sorry, too, Megan. I never meant to make you feel abandoned or like I didn't love you. I, of course, never wanted you to feel like you're not my little sister anymore, or like you're any less a part of my life and you ever were. I never meant to do that, and I'm so sorry you felt that way," I said. "I was trying to build my career. I thought you understood that."

"I did. I do. But that doesn't make it any less hard. I tried to do it all on my own, but I couldn't," Megan said, her head lowering. "I'm not as strong as you."

I looked at Toby.

"Help me up, please," I said.

Toby came over to the bad and carefully help me sit up. I swung my legs over the side, and he took my hands to bring me up to my feet. I couldn't move too far away from that position considering the IV was still in my arm, but I could open my arms up to my sister. Megan rushed to me and wrapped her arms around me. I held her close, stroking the back of her hair like I used to when she was a little girl. When the hug ended, I kept hold of her hand and looked between her and Toby.

"They're keeping me for the rest of the night. They won't release me until morning. There's no point in everyone staying here and being exhausted. The two of you should go get some rest," I told them.

"She's right," Toby agreed. "We're going to have to figure out how we're going to handle this tomorrow, and none of us are going to be any good if we haven't slept. Megan, you should go get some sleep, and I'll stay here with Maddie to make sure she's all right."

"No," I said, catching his flip even though he got the words out of his mouth as fast as possible. "You're going to go get some sleep, too. I'm sure Nurse Feelgood is going to come back in here any minute and pump me full of more of that sleepy-time juice. There won't be any point in either of you being here. Toby, you need to sleep, too. But, Megan, you can't go back to Craig's house. It isn't safe."

"He'll just come find me at the sorority house," she said. "He knows where it is, and they won't stop him from coming in."

She sounded worried, and I knew the reality of what had happened with Craig had settled in.

"I'll get her a room at the hotel where we're staying," Toby said. "She'll be safe there."

"Thank you," I said.

Seeing there was no point in arguing with me, Toby nodded. He leaned down to kiss me, and they walked out of the room, closing the door behind them. Finally alone, I sat on the bed, thinking about everything. I never could have imagined this was how things would have turned out. Not with my sister. Not with my career. Not with my personal life. Right then I knew all the plans I thought I'd had in place for my life had been completely thrown off track. Nothing was ever going to be the same, and I had to figure out where I was going to fall in all of it.

The longer I thought about it, the more I realized what had to be done. I couldn't leave my sister. Not with the way things were. I always knew she hated that I wasn't in Lawrence anymore and had moved to New York for my career, but it never occurred to me that she felt abandoned.

She was dramatic, certainly, and I constantly had to deal with her complaints and whining about everything she thought was going wrong in her life. But I never thought she actually felt like I had just left her behind, or that she couldn't get on without me. Now with everything she'd gone through with Craig, and the potential for much more to come, there was no way I could just go back to New York and let her fend for herself.

Beyond that, I couldn't just pretend nothing else was changing in my life. If I really was pregnant, I couldn't expect everything to stay the same at work. I would be the boss's pet, and no one would ever see me the same way. Toby might have been willing to be my fake husband, but he didn't say anything about being a real one. I loved him. It was hard to wrap my head around and even harder to admit. Somewhere in all this, in the hours I'd spent with him and the strong friendship we'd built, I'd fallen in love with Toby. But the whole situation was fucked, and I couldn't expect to bring him into it. He had a life back in New York, and I wasn't going to take him from it.

I thought there would be relief when I finally made a decision. Instead, it was just hurt and a sense of uncertainty and emptiness. But it was the right thing to do. I would stay in Kansas while Megan finished college. I would file a restraining order against Craig and encourage my sister to do the same on the grounds of the threats he'd made against her to me. This would at least give us recourse if he tried to come for either of us again. From there, I would find a job and focus on getting through this pregnancy and raising my baby. When Megan graduated, we would find some place new to live, together as a family, and figure out a new life.

It would hurt. There was no question not seeing Toby would be painful and leave a major hole in my life, but I couldn't expect him to just pick up and move to Kansas. He had a multimillion-dollar business to run and was just getting more successful by the day. That was his life, and I needed to let him live it.

Despite the pain and heartache to come, that night I fell asleep easily, knowing everything was settled and, one way or the other, it would work out.

The next morning, Toby showed up early, bringing a sleepy Megan along with him. I couldn't waste any time. The longer I delayed, the harder it would be to put the decisions I'd made the night before into action.

"So, before I'm discharged, I wanted to talk to both of you," I told them. "I did a lot of thinking last night and decided it would be best for me to stay here in Lawrence."

Megan's face glowed and she broke out into a huge smile, but Toby immediately looked shocked.

"Megan, do you think you could do me a huge favor and go to the cafeteria for some coffee? I haven't had a cup this morning and I'm really feeling it," he said.

He reached in his pocket and handed her several folded bills. She nodded and agreed, almost bouncing as she left. As soon as she was gone, he turned to me.

"What are you talking about?" he demanded. "You can't stay here. Your life is in New York."

"Toby, this is what I have to do. Megan needs me. You heard her. She can't do this without me," I pointed out.

"Your sister can transfer to a school in New York. That way you can keep her job, and she'll have the added benefit of being away from Craig," he said.

I shook my head. "It won't work. She will want to finish school and graduate with all her friends around her. The sorority is important to her, and she'll want to celebrate her accomplishment with people she knows rather than a bunch of strangers she only just met. I'm not going to uproot her while she's still in school." I took a deep breath. "I want to thank you for being such a good friend and for helping me through all this. But now that we've gotten the issue with Megan settled, I think it's time for a fake divorce."

"Are you sure that's what you really want?"

I wasn't, but there was no way I could tell him that. "Yes, it's what I really want."

I smiled at him hoping for one in return, but a hurt expression crossed Toby's face.

"I understand," he said, his tone emotionless. "I'll book myself a flight home."

CHAPTER 28

TOBY

I picked up the silver ball at the end of the row of hanging spheres, pulled it up, and dropped it for what was probably the hundredth time that day. It hit the next ball, causing the one on the end to bounce. I watched as the effect caused the balls to swing back and forth until they finally went still again. This had become a large part of my daily functioning. It had been three months since I'd left Lawrence, Kansas, to return to Manhattan alone. Three months of pure hell. I couldn't concentrate on my work. I couldn't eat. I barely slept. All I could do was miss Maddie. Everything I did made me think of her, and every time I thought of her, the pain was a little stronger. I didn't understand where everything had gone wrong and how we could have ended up in this place. Even before we left for Kansas, I was sure our relationship was moving forward. I told myself she was mine and there was no way I was going to let her go. But I had.

It seemed to mean nothing to her to tell me she was going to stay in Kansas with her sister rather than coming back to New York. She was completely willing to give up everything she'd worked hard to build in her career, and whatever we might have together, and didn't think twice about it.

Nik came into my office during a long stretch of me staring off into space. That was another of the new pastimes that took up a portion of my day. He walked in, turned slightly like he was trying to figure out what I was looking at so intently, and let out a sigh.

"Maddie is not up in that light fixture, Toby," he told me. "And I really don't think staring at a fluorescent bulb like that is great for your eyes. If you're going to continue to make this a part of your routine, I suggest you look into some specialized sunglasses."

"Yeah," I said with a groan as I closed my eyes and rubbed my lids with my fingertips. "I'll keep that in mind."

Nik let out a sigh and dropped down into the chair across the desk from me.

"You need to go after her already. Honestly, this is getting ridiculous, and you know as well as I do the only thing that's going to make it any better is if you're with Maddie again. I happen to speak from experience with this one. I didn't exactly react well to being away from Jane," he said.

"Yeah, I remember," I pointed out. "You were a serious asshole while she was gone."

He laughed but held out a hand like he was demonstrating evidence.

"And what did I do? I went to Paris and brought her home. No more asshole. You need to do the same. You're lost in this mopey world of not being good for shit, and it's all because Maddie isn't here with you. It's not like she's lost in the wild. You know where to find her. Go get her and bring her home," he said.

"Our situations are different," I told him. "She's not just off hiding from me in Kansas. She's supporting her younger sister. It's a lot more complicated."

Nik shook his head. "There is nothing complicated about this. You love her. You need to go after her. It's as simple as that."

He reached forward and dropped a folded newspaper onto the desk in front of me.

"What's this?" I asked. "This isn't going to be taking this thing full circle and I'm going to find Maddie's wedding announcement to Craig, am I?"

I was only partially kidding. The reality was Craig wasn't going to marry anybody anytime soon. At least, not if he didn't want the ceremony to be performed through a piece of glass. His trial for what he did to Maddie was coming up quickly, and there was no way he was getting out of the charges. Of course, he tried to convince both Megan and Maddie to let it drop. He put on a simpering display worthy of an Academy Award, then when that didn't work out for him, he tried a full-on temper tantrum. The only thing that succeeded in doing was getting him tossed into jail for a few days, the judge increasing his bond and issuing a very stern warning about him coming into contact with either one of them again.

"Not exactly," Nik said. "But it does have to do with Craig."

I picked up the newspaper and looked at it. It wasn't traditional news, the society pages, or even, despite my glimmer of hope, the obituaries. Instead, it was the sports section.

"What's this?" I asked.

"Just read it," Nik said.

I scanned the newspaper, trying to find any mention of Craig. Finally, I found it. The column was small, barely a collection of a few lines, but it was there. An announcement stating Craig Shelton, former assistant coach at KU, no longer had an offer to coach at Kansas State.

"Fantastic," I said, smiling for the first time in a long time.

"It's just a formality. He lost the opportunity a while ago, obviously. But it's still nice to see it in print, isn't it?" Nik asked.

"Yes, it is. I must admit, you were right. As much as I would have liked to take matters into my own hands, and by take matters into my own hands, of course, I mean throttling Craig, this is actually better. I didn't need to clobber him or find out what it's like to spend twenty-three hours of my day in a space not as big as my current closet, but he still went down," I said.

"And it will just keep getting better," Nik promised. "This is just one phase of the public humiliation portion of his restitution for what he did to Maddie and what he threatened to do to Megan. He might have figured out a way to post bail and get out while awaiting trial, but with all the evidence and Maddie, Megan, and you testifying, he's looking at some very hard time. Attempted murder is no joke. Even if he can charm his way into getting jury to recommend a lesser charge, he's still looking at years for aggravated assault. And when he does finally get out, it definitely won't be to a hero's welcome."

"I take it you had that meeting with the athletic director of KU?" I asked.

"Yes, I did. They knew about the charges pending against Craig, of course, but I made sure to pinpoint for them exactly what those charges were based on. And just in case that wasn't enough for them, I let them know they should separate themselves from him based on moral grounds, namely dating students. They not only agreed wholeheartedly but assured me they would be speaking to their entire network to make sure everyone has a clear and honest depiction of who Craig is."

"Thank you for doing that for me, and for Maddie," I said.

"Absolutely. That's what friends are for. Besides, I'm not about to let a scumbag like him get away with the kind of shit he pulled," Nik said. "But none of you will have to deal with him again. If he puts one more toe out of line, he's going to end up in jail until his trial. Then after the trail, he'll be in prison for years to come. And then after that... well, I don't care what the fuck happens to him after that. He'll have to figure that out for himself. All that matters is he won't be bothering Maddie or Megan anymore."

Before he could launch back into another campaign for me to go after Maddie, the door to my office pushed the rest of the way open and Jane popped her head in.

"So, this is where you're hiding," she said.

"Not fair. You didn't count to at least one hundred before you came looking for me," Nik teased.

Jane smiled and came into the room. Their little baby, Rose, was in her arms.

"Well, I won, anyway." She kissed him. "I actually have a meeting. You're going to have to handle the baby for an hour or two."

Nik's face lit up, and he reached for his daughter.

"I am more than happy to do so," he said. "Come here, princess. We never get to hang out enough, do we?"

He cuddled the baby close to him, and Jane smiled. I

watched them, a feeling of pure envy in my heart. I couldn't help but wish that were Maddie and me. The little family looked so happy, so contented. Seeing it was the final straw. Maybe Nik was right.

I didn't even bother to pack a bag. As soon as work was over, I went straight to the airport. I was going to win Maddie back, even if I had to move to Kansas to do it.

CHAPTER 29

MADDIE

The late afternoons seemed to hit me harder those days. It was right around three and I was sitting at my desk, trying to keep my mind focused on my work, but I was distracted. My energy was dragging, leaving my body feeling like it was being weighed down by sandbags. Getting used to the extra baby weight wasn't helping, but it was mostly just the sheer tiredness of my second trimester getting to me. I never felt like I could eat enough to keep myself feeling full or to give me enough energy to get through my day. No matter how much I slept at night, right around this time every day, I was tired enough to just put my head down and sleep. There had been days when I was tempted to smuggle a pillow and blanket under my desk and hide under there for naps.

That probably wouldn't have been in good form, considering I had only been working at my new job for the past two months. It definitely wasn't as exciting as my last job, and it often left my mind vulnerable to wandering around, delving into thoughts I shouldn't be thinking. But the pay was decent, and the people I was working with were nice enough. I wasn't going to pretend that had been all smooth and rosy. In fact, it had been a rough transition I hadn't always been sure I would be able to navigate, but my relationship with Megan was getting better every day. The closer bond we were experiencing helped on the days when the stark contrast between my life in New York and my life here in Kansas became so much I didn't know if I would ever find my way again. Megan and I hadn't been this truly close in years, and that helped carry me through. I told myself eventually I'd find the right groove. I'd figure it all out again just like I had when I first moved to New York, and I'd feel like I was living my own life again rather than borrowing it from someone else.

But there was one thing that always stayed with me. No matter how much I pushed behind me and how much I looked ahead, I couldn't stop thinking about Toby. I was missing him like crazy. The pregnancy hormones weren't helping. Every little thing got me emotional, and with those emotions came more longing for Toby. I wanted him to experience all these little things with me, all the changes and the milestones. I wasn't looking forward to going through all of it alone. Megan was being incredibly supportive and was so excited about welcoming her little niece or nephew into the world in a few months. But that wasn't the same as sharing it with the baby's father. The man I loved.

Maybe I should call him. That debate went through my head a few times a week. I wondered if I'd done the right thing, or if I should have been up-front with him from the very beginning. Maybe it wasn't too late. I could give in and call him. I could tell him what happened and explain my reasoning but tell him I want him to be a part of it now. If he wanted to be, of course.

Almost as if the thinking about making a phone call willed my phone into action, it rang. I jumped slightly and reached for it, hoping my voice wasn't shaking it when I answered. I was surprised when I heard the receptionist tell me if someone was at the front desk wanting it to see me.

"Is it my sister?" I asked.

Megan had gotten into the habit of occasionally dropping by the office to bring snacks or update me on her day. She was really applying herself and working hard. Though I knew the primary motivation behind her visits was to check in on me and make sure I was doing well, it was also a form of accountability for her. But the receptionist said it wasn't her. Even more surprised and wondering who it could possibly be, I thanked her and said I was on my way down. I took a swig from the water bottle on my desk and headed for the lobby. As I approached the front desk, I was shocked to see Toby standing there. My mind went straight to being thankful that I wore a flowy dress that day. It hid my growing baby bump, preventing it from being at the first thing he noticed about me.

"Toby," I said. "What are you doing here?"

He came toward me. "I needed to see you."

"How did you know where I was?" I asked. "I haven't told anybody where I'm working now. Not even Jane."

"That's not exactly true," Toby pointed out. "You asked Ethan for a reference."

I cringed slightly, remembering a somewhat awkward phone conversation to the marketing director. He promised to remain discreet, but apparently didn't think that extended to telling Toby about the reference and glowing recommendation he'd made for me when I was applying for this job.

"Oh, yeah. I did that, didn't I?" I asked. "It figures he would tell you."

Toby shrugged and gave me a slightly awkward smile.

"I have my ways of getting the information I want. I really need to talk to you."

I stared at him for a few long seconds.

"Let me go grab my things, and I'll leave a little early for the day," I told him. "We can grab some coffee nearby and catch up."

Toby nodded and I left him in the lobby to go back to my office. I tried not to let myself think too much as I gathered my belongings and shut things down for the day. I didn't really know why he was there or what his intentions were. As much as I wanted to see him and to know he was still thinking about me as much as I was thinking about him, it was entirely possible there was a different explanation. I'd left the company so abruptly, I dropped out of a major project. Maybe he was just there to ask me questions about it and find out about the plans I'd made. And even if he was there to see me, I didn't know how he was going to react to everything going on. But I couldn't delay it anymore. He was waiting for me.

He smiled at me when I walked back into the lobby, and I had the compulsion to run into his arms. I wanted to feel him hold me, to be able to breathe in the smell of him. Instead, I kept my distance, and we walked down a few doors to a little coffee shop I'd gotten familiar with since getting the job. Toby ordered coffee, and before he could order the same for me, I asked for a decaffeinated tea. He looked at me strangely, knowing that wasn't my style, but didn't say anything.

"What did you want to talk about?" I asked as he walked over to one of the small tables and sat down.

He looked at me, seeming to be struggling with his thoughts.

"I love you," he suddenly blurted out. "I miss you, Maddie. I can't live without you anymore. I tried. I did everything I possibly could to figure out life without you in it, but I just can't. I know none of this sounds good, and I probably sound pathetic, but the truth is, I've never wanted a woman more than I want you. I know there are some things standing in our way, but I'm willing to do whatever it takes to be with you. Hell, I'll even relocate my company to Kansas. Or sell the whole damn thing to Nik and start over here."

The burst of emotion and revelation shocked me so much I wasn't sure how to respond. I should have approached it logically and calmly. Instead, I let everything inside me take over.

"I love you, too," I said without thinking. "I've missed you so much. But I'm not sure how we can make things work."

Toby reached across the table and grabbed my hands.

"We'll figure it out together." He looked around. "Let's get out of here. I have a hotel nearby. Go there with me. I need to feel you in my arms."

I nodded and we rushed out of the coffee shop to the hotel. Getting there and through the lobby to the room was a blur. All my mind could process was that I was with Toby again. He was right here with me, and he loved me.

The door to the room wasn't even closed all the way before Toby's hands were in my hair and he pushed me back up against the door, kissing me passionately. I kissed him back hungrily, running my hands over his shoulders and down his back and savoring his body near mine again. His hands moved to my clothes, starting to undress me, and reality hit.

"Stop," I said.

Toby pulled back, looking worried.

"What's wrong?" he asked.

"Nothing. I just need to tell you something, and I hope it won't change everything."

"There's nothing you could tell me that would change the way I feel about you."

"Toby, I'm pregnant."

His mouth fell open, his reaction clearly shocked.

"I can't believe it," he said.

Deciding he needed some irrefutable reality, I pulled my dress up and displayed my bump. Fear that he would get angry coursed through me. I waited for him to yell, to pull away and tell me he didn't want to see me anymore. Instead, his face broke into a huge smile.

"This is incredible," he said.

He dropped to his knees and kissed my belly, stroking his hands over it. In that instant, I fell even more in love with him.

Slowly, he kissed up my body, finding what skin was exposed and covering it with his touch, reaching my neck before stepping back and pausing. In that pause, time seemed to still, and my vision filled with only him. He leaned in and our lips touched, and months of hunger and pain and loneliness and worry all melted away. He was here now, where he belonged, his lips on mine, and his hands sliding around me, pulling me into him with his firm grip.

I reached up and pulled at his tie, loosening it enough

that I could grab one side and yank it, unraveling it and letting it drop to the floor. Trembling fingers unbuttoned his shirt, and my breath hitched as his lips moved back down to my neck again. I rolled my head to the side to give him better access as my fingers worked quickly on his shirt. His hands slid down my sides and grasped for the edge of my dress, pulling it up until he had to stop kissing me long enough to bring it over my head. When it was off me, he let it drop from his fingers to the floor. I reached behind me and unclasped my bra, and his eager hands rose to remove the cups off my heaving breasts. He lifted the bra up and they dropped heavily from it, bouncing playfully, until his palms filled with them.

With my chest bare, I guided him to the bed, making him sit. I knelt to the ground, pulling my knees under myself, and unhooked his belt. He made a movement to get me off the ground, but I put my hand on his chest to stop him. His desire to protect me, to keep me from being uncomfortable, was endearing and loving, but I was fine. I wanted this. I unhooked the clasp of his pants and pulled them down until he had to move so they would come off. His cock was hard inside his boxers, and I salivated at the thought of it finally being free. I trailed kisses up his thigh as one hand ran up his chest and the other reached for his waistband. He rose to help me remove the underwear, and as it slid off his chiseled core, it revealed the deep v of his muscles and the thick, long cock that I had missed so much.

I took him in my hand and stroked him slowly, positioning myself so that the head was pushing against my chest. Toby's mouth was open, and heavy breath came from his chest as he focused on my touch. I squeezed my shoulders forward and wrapped his girth between my breasts, and he moaned loudly. I reveled in that sound, knowing it was my touch that brought him to this level of delight. I pushed my breasts together and used them to stroke him, occasionally dipping my head down to lick the slick wet tip. After a few moments, his hand slipped behind my head and guided me until I took him entirely into my mouth.

I nearly came the second her mouth wrapped tightly around me, but I held fast, wanting to extend the pleasure as long as possible. I had waited for her touch, to touch her, to place my lips on her skin for so long. And now, my cock was surrounded by the warm, wet grip of her mouth, and I had to fight losing control almost immediately. She stroked me as she worshipped me with her tongue, sliding it up and down along the veins and ridges of my cock, and I gripped the edge of the bed to maintain some measure of control. It was not a hurried rhythm, but a deliberate one. Maddie was showing me, with every stroke, how much she had missed me, too.

Releasing me, Maddie looked up into my eyes and smiled. I couldn't help but return a grin, and I gently pulled her up by her shoulders. It was my turn to place her on the bed, and I knelt before her, kissing down the side of her body until I reached her leggings. I pulled them down, revealing delicate white panties underneath and tossed the leggings aside. I traced my tongue up her thigh and blew a stream of warm air on the slick mark, watching as goose-bumps covered her delicate skin. Her hands found my hair and grabbed handfuls of it as I traced my way along the edge of the panties, fingers hooking in the waistband and slowly peeling them away.

Soon, her pussy was revealed to me, and I drew my thumb across the lips, finding the center and applying a tiny bit of pressure. She writhed happily underneath my touch, and I rolled the pad of my thumb as her legs opened further to give me complete access. I brushed my tongue across her center, and she moaned deeply. Two fingers sat at the edge of her opening and slid in as I pressed my tongue into her clit. The fingers in my hair tightened, and a short burst of sound came from deep inside her as I started to push the fingers in and out in rhythm with the movements of my tongue. It didn't take long before her hitching breath told me her body was ready to release, and I increased the speed. The staccato moans exploded into one long sound, and her body shook, her thighs closing around my ears and her fingers reaching for my chin to pull me up to her.

She needed me inside her as much as I needed to be there, but I didn't want to rush it. I wanted to enjoy this reunion, and I plunged into her immediately but held it there, letting her wriggle and writhe around me. When her body calmed, I placed my hands on her hips and pulled her to me, so her ass was almost off the edge of the bed. I rocked myself back and then forward again in slow, long move-ments, bending over to place my mouth on her skin.

I trailed kisses across her chest, taking her sensitive nipples in my mouth one at a time and flicking them with my tongue. When they were wet and peaked, I blew a stream of hot breath on them and watched as the skin around it reacted. My thrusts became harder, though I didn't increase the speed. I wanted to explore her, and let her feel the length of me, without worry about finishing too soon. I never wanted to leave the comfort and warmth of her body and would stay buried deeply in her pussy as long as I could.

Maddie reached up, wrapping her arms around my neck and pulling herself up. For a moment, I stood, supporting her weight entirely and lifting her to bounce gently on my cock. She reveled in the new position for a moment, her eyes closing tightly before opening again and meeting me with a deep, longing kiss.

"Lay down," she whispered as our lips parted, and I carried her onto the bed without removing myself from inside her. We wiggled until my head was on the pillows and she rested on top of me. Placing her hands on my chest, she gently stroked me, rocking her hips back and forth again in an even, measured motion. Soon we had fallen into a comfortable rhythm, enjoying our bodies and letting our fingers explore each other, our lips closing over whatever body part it could reach.

I sat up, clasping her close to me, one hand on the back of her hip and guiding her motions, the other reaching up into her hair and gently holding her by the back of her head, pushing her into another deep kiss. Her speed increased as our foreheads touched, and I could tell she was closing in on another orgasm. I let myself get lost in the moment, no longer holding myself back from release, and could feel the build of the moment coming. Her moans became short and higher-pitched again, and her head rocked back as she shouted to the sky the sounds of her ecstasy.

I put both hands on her ass and guided her to get faster, harder with her motions. Her moans got louder, less controlled, more desperate, and I felt myself riding the wave with her. A sudden rush of adrenaline and passion and need coursed through me, and I pulled her hard, slamming her body over mine, thrusting deeply inside her with each pull. Her fingers dug into my back, and she suddenly went stock-still, and I exploded into her. I came hard, my body vibrating with a blinding orgasm that left me incapable of sound or thought or control. I sat with her pulsing on top of me, milking me deeply into her body, with my mouth agape. The world faded back into view as I came down from the feeling, and Maddie collapsed into my arms, her body spent.

Gently, I lay back, holding her close to me, and pulled the sheets over us. We lay like that for some time, as our bodies gently returned to our control.

No moment in my life had ever been as perfect as that one as I lay in the hotel bed with Maddie in my arms. I realized as I cradled her to me, holding her tight like I was never going to let her go, but right here, in my arms, I had everything I could ever want. Never had I felt more satisfied or fulfilled. Maddie was right here with me. She loved me, and she was going to have my baby. It was all so incredible. We lay there in silence for several seconds before she nestled closer.

"What made you come back?" she asked. "I've been here for three months. What prompted you to come back now?"

I leaned down and kissed her on the top of the head.

"Every day of those three months I was miserable. I kept telling myself things were going to get better and everything was going to work out eventually, but that eventually never came. Nothing made me feel better. Even telling myself this was what you wanted and reminding myself we never had a discussion about being in a real relationship did nothing. I just kept thinking about you and missing you more and more. I wanted to give you what you thought was right, but it was ripping me apart. And seeing how happy Nik and Jane are with their baby finally convinced me. If they were able to make it work, then maybe you and I could. So, I came after you," I told her.

"I'm so glad you did," she said. "I've been missing you so much and wishing you were here with me. I know I said this is the way I wanted it to be, but it never felt right. I'm so happy you're here now. But what do we do?"

"What do you mean? I asked.

"The whole reason I stayed here was to take care of and make sure Megan got through school. I didn't want her to quit school or get more overwhelmed and end up making more bad decisions. She still has a couple of months left until graduation. She's doing really well, and she's almost done. I can't derail her now," Maddie said.

I didn't even hesitate.

"It's fine. I'll stay here in Lawrence with the two of you. I can work remotely. I may have to fly to New York occasionally for important meetings, but you are far more important than any job or company." I ran my hand over the swell of her belly. "Both of you are."

"I can't believe you'd do that for me," she said.

"Of course I would. You're worth it," I told her.

"I hope you still feel that way after a couple months living with Megan," Maddie said.

I laughed.

"I'd put up with a million bratty sisters for you," I told her.

Maddie kissed me. Everything she would ever need to say was in that kiss. It was everything. I'd never been more fulfilled and complete. This was unlike anything I'd ever experienced in my life, and it could only get better from here. I couldn't wait to experience it all.

Even a year after coming back from Kansas, being in New York still felt wonderful every day. It was like having to be away from it for those several months gave me a new appreciation for the city. I'd gotten so used to it after living there for the years after leaving home the first time that I no longer noticed all the little things about it that made me fall in love with it from the beginning. I knew there was something special about New York, and it was where I felt like my life had really begun but having to be away from it brought back the spark and adoration. Even a year later, it hadn't faded, and I didn't think it ever would. Life was nowhere near close to what it was when I first showed up in New York from Kansas, and every day there was something new and exciting to discover or experience.

I followed in Jane's footsteps, refusing to compromise when it came to both my career and my family. Just because I was with Toby and he could afford to completely take care of me and our son and give us a luxurious, indulged life didn't mean I was just going to automatically give up my career. I'd worked hard to get to where I was, to prove myself enough to work in the marketing department of Toby's company to begin with. But I also loved what I did. I enjoyed working and spending time with the other members of the marketing department. I was proud of what we'd come up with together and the incredible success of the launches we'd designed over the last couple of years. I didn't want that to go away. Especially now that I had a new title.

I was no longer just the assistant marketing director. That was Jane's position, now. After getting an exceptional offer, and with Toby's full blessing, Ethan left and went to work for another company. That left his position open, and I was promoted to marketing director. I wouldn't say it had always been an easy and smooth transition. It was hard work, and there was a lot of learning to be done. But I loved growing into the role and knew I was doing a good job. Along with my new assistant director, Jane, I was working on a new campaign for the spin-off to the app launched the year before. That was the first campaign she and I worked on together, and it had been a tremendous success. Working together again on the successor of the app felt natural and also thrilling. I couldn't wait to see what else this role would bring into my life.

But it wasn't just my career I was devoted to. As much as I wasn't willing to give up my career at Toby's company, I also wasn't going to compromise on my devotion to my family. Toby and Harrison were everything to me, and I wanted to give them as much of myself as I possibly could. I was the ultimate example of the woman who wanted it all. And I wasn't going to settle for anything less. Fortunately, I didn't have to.

Ever since Jane came back from Paris, heavily pregnant with her and Nik's daughter, Rose, the office had become an extremely baby-friendly place. At first, I loved it because it gave me the opportunity to enjoy the last bit of Jane's pregnancy with her, then get in plenty of quality baby cuddle time with Rose. Now I adored it because it gave me the opportunity to bring my own son to work with me every day. I never had to be away from him or worry about him being taken care of by anyone else. I got to experience all his little moments and not be concerned that I wouldn't be around for one of his milestones. It also meant Toby got to spend more time with him, and it made our family even stronger.

Speaking of family, it wasn't just the three of us back in New York. True to our plan, as soon as Megan graduated from KU, she packed up and left Kansas to join us in the Big Apple. She was surprisingly nervous just before and during the move. I figured with as much as she loved the partying lifestyle when she was in Kansas, she would adore being in a bigger, more intense city. But my sister worried she wasn't going to fit in or that the faster pace and more dynamic surroundings would swallow her up.

Fortunately, that fear didn't last long. Within just a few weeks of her arriving here and Toby and I setting her up in her own apartment, she really found her stride. She woke up in a way I didn't expect, and it seemed like my little sister had finally really found herself. It absolutely thrilled her when Toby told her he'd found Megan an internship at a company owned by his friend Devin McKay. She was happy as a clam and adjusting to her new life beautifully. I rarely ever heard her complain anymore, and even when I did, it was almost endearing. It was just part of who my sister was. And after coming face-to-face with the possibility of losing her, it made me appreciate her and her little idiosyncrasies even more.

Most of the time. There were still instances when she drove me up a wall and I had to convince her she really could do this on her own. Sometimes it took a reminder of what she'd been through and how strong she'd been to get her back on track. But I had absolute faith in her. I knew she put the negative things about herself behind her and was ready for a new life.

I had just finished packing Harrison's diaper bag when Toby walked into the office. He smiled at me and reached down into the playpen to stroke our son's face.

"Are you almost ready?" he asked. "It's almost time for Nik and Jane's anniversary dinner."

"I'm ready," I told him.

"Good. The restaurant is close by. Do you want to just walk there together?" Toby asked.

I smiled and scooped the baby out from the playpen to settle him into his stroller. He continued to sleep, looking peaceful and perfect in the shade of the stroller canopy.

"I will always walk anywhere with you," I told Toby.

He wrapped his arms around my waist and pulled me up close for a deep kiss. I could have just stayed right there in that moment and been perfectly happy. But there was a celebration going on, and we wanted to be a part of it. Toby took the handles of the stroller and pushed as we made our way out of the office and down the block toward the restaurant. Selfishly, I wanted to go slower, to take in every second and experience all of it.

When we arrived at the restaurant, our friends were smiling and happy, enjoying being together. I looked at Toby and felt my heart swell. I had gotten everything I wanted. My life was perfect now, and it was only just beginning.

The End